A Curiosity

The Last Straw

Aelfraed

Warnings: This story contains manipulative family members, descriptions of burns and bloody wounds.

Emmy Wynn Galloway

This is a work of fiction. While the setting may feature familiar aspects being based in an alternate universe of our world, characters, names, incidents and places are products of the author's imagination or are used fictitiously. Any resemblance to actual persons and events is entirely coincidental. Any resemblance to places is rather the point but they are used fictitiously.

Copyright © Emmy Wynn Galloway, 2023

All rights reserved. No part of this book may be reproduced in any form by electronic or mechanical means, including information storage and retrieval systems, without permission in writing from the copyright holder, except by a reviewer who may quote brief passages in a review.

Illustrations © Emmy Wynn Galloway, 2023
Cover design by Britt Coxon

This paperback edition was first published in 2023

ISBN Paper Back 978-1-7384477-1-8
ISBN E-Book 978-1-7384477-0-1

Independently published by Emmy Wynn Galloway of Masked Emerald Creations
www.MaskedEmerald.co.uk

Timeline

Aelfraed starts at the university.

The Medallion Heist
A cursed item is stolen from the museum and it isn't the first, Aelfraed is dragged into the case.

The Last Straw
Aelfraed leaves university after breaking under the stress and finds himself having a rather unlucky weekend.

Aelfraed becomes a detective officially.

Chapter One

Aelfraed had been hearing the snapping of metaphorical threads for weeks, the weight of years of pressure pulling on him. Stretching, fibres fraying. He was about to break. He lay in his bed staring at the door, grimacing with the passing of any footsteps. Breath held as he waited for the clunk of a turning door handle. He just wanted to be left alone.

He had stumbled into the room hours ago. Kicking off his shoes between the door and the bed. They still lay there abandoned on the floor. He had dropped onto the bed without changing. His once neat shirt now crumpled awkwardly underneath him, the belt of his trousers digging into his stomach and side. He was dreading the morning, the intensive studying that would come. Dreading the exam, the one he had failed once. The one he would fail again before he even started to study. He didn't deserve the second chance that his father had fought for. He wasn't sure he wanted it. What good was he? The pressure was too much. The pressure of being made to fit a mould that wasn't him. Pushed and shoved, he would fit or break. He was breaking.

He forced himself up, he needed to get away. Just a break. A break and then, then he would be fine. His father wouldn't like it but he couldn't take it. He needed time away, just a few days. He couldn't have that time with his father breathing down his neck. A couple of days just to be him again. Then he'd come back.

He found his case buried and unused since the day he arrived at the bottom of the wardrobe. He packed a few sets of clothing, not too much. Nothing that would stand out as gone, if someone came looking for him before the morning. Just a few simple shirts, woollen cardigans, a tightly woven overcoat set to one side. He paused as he closed the case, eyeing the stack of books on his bedside. He should take them, even just one but he didn't want to. It was a weight both physically and mentally that he didn't need. It was only going to be a couple of days, right? He'd be fine without; he'd be subjected to his father's intensive sessions when he got back regardless.

He slipped on his discarded shoes and threw on the long caped coat he had set to one side. He picked up the case as he brushed his hand over the simple glowing engraving on the bedside table. The glow dimmed at his touch and faded out entirely in the few steps it took to get to the door.

The door creaked as he opened it, he winced but the corridor stayed empty. He stepped softly, careful not to disturb anyone that was still awake. Once he was out in the dark of the cold night it was easy to blend in with the evening crowds on the streets. At such a late hour the carriage stand towards the edge of the city was almost deserted. Little other than the few who were in need of an extra trip in their ledger.

"Where you heading lad?" the man Aelfraed approached asked.

That made Aelfraed pause, he hadn't planned this far. He hadn't considered where he was going, just not in the city. Only one place sprung to mind, Newcastle. Fortunately the coins in his pocket were enough to get him there, hopefully it wouldn't be a bad time to visit.

Chapter Two

Hours later, rain rolled down the glass of the carriage window. It drummed rhythmically off the roof that was far closer to Aelfraed's head than he would have liked. The space cramped with his height. It was still preferable to the Rune Step. The Step would have been faster, instant even, but he had always found it unpleasant. Even more so over longer distances. He shifted trying to get a bit more comfortable, nothing really helped much. He did manage to stop himself hitting his head off of the ceiling with every bump in the road. Still not enough to find the sleep he half wished he had been able to get before leaving. His eyes were heavy and the bumps were the only thing keeping him from it.

Every time he drifted he was shaken harshly out of it.

Behind the dark rain clouds the sky was lightening by the time he clambered out of the carriage, his stiff limbs protesting after hours in the cramped space. He stretched, reaching for the sky feeling the stiffness leave his back before foraging through pockets. His hands found his remaining few coins, a fountain pen and some scribbled notes but not the pocket watch he was looking for. He had forgotten it; he could almost see the watch in his bedside drawer. That was just his luck at the moment. He glanced towards the sky, blinking against the falling rain. He wasn't sure but if his brother wasn't awake yet, he would be soon. With how light it was, it couldn't be that early that it would be an uncomfortable hour at this time of year.

The carriage rolled off behind him as he lifted his hand above his head, muttering a short few words of a spell. Willing a shimmering barrier into existence, like a fountain from his hand. Rain rolled down it and poured off the sides. It took a few steps to shake out the stiffness in his gait. He tried to step carefully to avoid any muddy puddles. The runes carved into the soles of his shoes would keep his feet dry, but he didn't want to accidentally end up tracking mud into his brother's house.

He carefully navigated the crowds that were growing in the streets as people got started with their day. Many like him had their hands raised above their heads to hold up shimmering barriers, the rain running off them. Others had items embroidered with repelling runes, hats and other such that saved them the need to cast the spell themselves. The odd carriage trundled past over the cobbles and outside the Rune Step points there was a constant flow of people going in and out.

It took a while for him to gain his bearings as he crossed the city. He was only vaguely familiar with the city from previous visits. Eventually he managed to find his way to familiar streets, quieter having moved against the grain of the crowd. The street was lined with terraced tall narrow houses that almost looked squished against each other. Three stories with a sheltered wooden porch sitting out from the house. A mix of wood and smoothed stone brickwork. The familiar house didn't stand out as much as it would have in warmer months, in those months the window-boxes below each sill would have been overflowing with flowers. Most were empty of all but soil now, the odd leafy plant still green. No attempt to extend their season with magic.

He walked the few steps that it took to cross the small paved and walled garden to the door. As he stepped up onto the doorstep another barrier sprung into visibility. It was flush against the door to the point where the red brown wooden door seemed to flicker and shimmer with a delicate blue. He knocked lightly on the door, his hand barely making contact with the surface. The sound was a muffled series of taps. Fortunately it didn't matter; the knock was more habit than necessary. Something he had picked up from visiting the offices at the university during various professors' open hours. Just stepping up to the door would have anyone inside aware that he was there.

The door opened with little more than a fizzle as the barrier vanished, and he was met with the smiling but confused face of his brother Aethelric looking up at him. Between them the height was the most obvious difference. They shared a rather pointed nose, Aethelric's face was slightly rounder but not by much leaving them both with narrow pointed faces. Their hair curly and dusty brown, well his brother's hair would have been curly if it wasn't brushed back and held that way with a touch of elixir. Instead it was tidy and smooth. Aelfraed personally preferred Aethelric's warm brown eyes over his own cold ice blue.

"Aelfie? What are you doing here?" he asked, glancing up the path behind Aelfraed, half expecting someone else, their father probably. As he did so he was hastily pulling on a smart woven tailed jacket. It matched the dark grey brown of Aethelric's trousers but contrasted with the rather bright amber colour of his shirt.

"I'm sorry, I just needed to get away for a bit. I can... I can find somewhere else to stay if you are..." Aelfraed was glad to not have woken him but he looked like he was on his way out. He didn't want to delay him over this.

The confused expression on Aethelric's face fell, a small frown forming. "No, no, none of that. Aelfie, you don't need to apologise and you most certainly don't need to go anywhere else. Come on in, I'll get us something to drink," he gestured for Aelfraed to follow him into the house.

Aelfraed followed tentatively. "Ah, no, Ric, you don't need to do that. I don't want to keep you."

Aethelric smiled back at him. "Stop worrying, I assure you it can wait. I was not in that much of a hurry. They'll survive without me for a while," he insisted as the door closed itself behind Aelfraed, he wasn't sure he believed him.

Aelfraed flicked his wrist and dropped his focus on the barrier above him. With a simple command and a flowing movement of his hand, he pulled the water that had reached his clothes out and into a plant pot that stood in the corner of the tiled foyer. He hung his jacket and slipped off his shoes before stepping up onto the dark stained wooden hallway floor. Aethelric took his case from his hand and set it down by the narrow staircase in a way of saying that he was staying. He guided

Aelfraed into the drawing room; it had barely changed since Aethelric had moved in. Books lined the walls. A fireplace crackled and warmed the room, plush armchairs and a settee crowded around it. Squished in another corner was a writing desk scattered with letters and ink bottles. Aethelric crouched in front of the fire placing a kettle amongst the flames with a gloved hand.

Aelfraed sat awkwardly in one of the armchairs and his brother took another. It was strange sitting in the armchair, despite his lankiness he felt too small in the chair that was usually reserved for their father. At least he knew Aethelric wouldn't protest but he still half expected his father to suddenly appear to chastise him. If the man appeared, being chastised about a chair would be the least of his worries his thoughts reminded him.

"So, I take it things are not going well at university?" Aethelric asked, not hesitating to get right to the issue. Aelfraed wished he had just acted like this was just a normal visit, just for a little bit.

He knew he would have to face it and talk sooner or later but he just wanted to forget for a bit. He eyed the kettle, it would still be a few minutes. Could he manage to put off the conversation that long? He picked at his trousers and tapped on the arm of the chair.

Aelfraed sighed; he was going to have to give in. The silence between them was leaving him with only the negative thoughts rattling in his head. "You have no idea, it's been a nightmare. Father has been… he's been worse since you left. Then university happened and he's…" he paused, slumping in the chair. It wasn't easy with the firm back. "He won't leave me be, pushing. Looking over my shoulder at every moment. I feel more like a puppet than me anymore. I can't even take a moment away from my studies for anything, even just to read something other than a textbook, not even one of a different subject. Maybe he was right to do that because now… now I've messed up…" maybe even again, maybe he shouldn't have come.

"Wait? How is he managing that? Father doesn't have that much influence," Aethelric stared at him, almost spilling the tea he was pouring. It took a moment for the smell of chamomile to hit him across the table. "You did manage to move out into the dormitories didn't you?"

"If only being in the dormitories would be enough to deter him. He's got himself appointed head of the department. Did it practically the week I applied, didn't know till I got there. He's been using it to watch my every move," it had been quite the shock; Aelfraed had been looking forward to the independence only to have it ripped out from under him. Even worse his father had kept it secret when the achievement would usually have been bragged about for months.

There was a frown on Aethelric's face. "Seriously, I knew he was overbearing but to go that far? I mean you were already doing everything he wanted to start with." He paused. "Aelfie? Please tell me you actually wanted to study to be a physician. Please tell me he at least let you choose for yourself what you wanted to do. Oh I should have asked earlier... much earlier."

"It's not your fault, I didn't know what I wanted. I just wanted to be better, to make up for not being good enough..." He sipped on the tea.

"Oh Aelfie, no. You don't have to make up for anything. What happened wasn't your fault, we were just kids."

Aelfraed tensed, he didn't want to talk about that. He shook his head. "I... please, can we not. I just need some time, I won't impose on you for long," even so many years later he was still raw, they all were.

"Aelfie, I'm sorry. Stay as long as you need," he said firmly. "However long you need to clear your head. However long it takes for you to work out what you want."

Aelfraed shook his head. "I can't, I'll get you into trouble. It's just another one of my mistakes. He'll know I'm gone soon. I just need a couple of days... then I'll go back," he didn't want to pit his brother against their father, not for him.

Aethelric sighed. "Fine, as I said, however long you want."

Chapter Three

The cold sun was dazzling bright the next morning as it streamed in through the guest bedroom window. It fell across his face slowly bringing him round from sleep. He lay there for a while. Not being sure if he wanted to get up yet, staring up at the wooden slats. He was still tired after crashing for most of the remainder of yesterday. He hadn't slept well. Even now he kept expecting his father to burst through the door demanding he get up, demanding he return immediately. He wasn't used to this quiet. It probably took an hour for him to drag himself out of bed.

He slipped down the stairs feeling awkward without his brother there. There was the sound of quick footsteps from behind him. His brother's wife Caoimhe was barrelling down the stairs, her hand dragging her long brown hair into a hasty ponytail. Her face was firm with focus.

He flattened against the wall as she bustled past, "Thanks Aelfraed," she said quickly as she passed.

She hit the bottom step and kept going, "Feeling any better this morning? Aethelric said you were having a bad time," she asked as she buttoned up the top button of her eggshell blue shirt.

"Maybe a little," he lied as he followed her down slowly, trying to keep out of the way. He didn't want to distract her with worry about him anyway either.

She hopped on one foot as she started pulling on her shin length boots. The boots were dark and shiny with polish but looked well worn. She gave a little smile as she finished lacing them up.

"That's good to hear," she pulled her coat down from the hook, "I'm sorry to do this, I know you were after a break but could you go into town and get me a few things. I was going to do it myself but they need me down the office. So much for a day off," she smiled and shook her head.

He could do that. A little shopping was fine. The request eased how guilty he felt just turning up out of the blue. At least he could do something to make his presence less of a burden. He shouldn't think like that, Aethelric would have said.

"No it's no bother. What do you need?" he asked.

She popped out her pocket watch from the pocket of her tailored navy blazer and glanced at the time. She breathed a sigh.

"Aethelric made a list of what we needed. It's on his desk," she said as she opened the door, a draft of cold air coming past her, "I'm sorry, I really have to get going. Just do what you can. We'll manage."

She rushed off leaving her keystone on the inside of the door before letting it close. Aelfraed shifted awkwardly in the silence. If the house had been off before in the complete silence it was more so. The liminality of somewhere without the people expected to be there. It made him feel like he shouldn't be there.

Aelfraed let out a long breath, at least now he had something to do for the day. A distraction of some kind. He headed through to the drawing room where Aethelric's desk stood squished into the corner. He tried not look at any of the assorted papers while still trying to locate the shopping list. He snatched it up when he spotted the list and put it in his pocket.

He considered heading out then and there without pause for even a late breakfast. It wasn't a good idea. He was already hungry and knew it would only bother Aethelric if he noticed that Aelfraed had skipped. He slipped into the kitchen and set about sorting out a late breakfast. Nothing complex and nothing that took him anywhere near the stove set against the wall.

He cleaned up after himself before setting out. Aelfraed moved about the kitchen, wiping down the benches and washing the small number of dishes remaining from breakfast. There wasn't much to do but it would make things easier on Aethelric and Caoimhe when they got home.

* * *

He stepped outside, tapping the keystone that had been set aside for him to the door frame. The rainwater from the day before still stood in puddles, slowly drying in the cold sunshine. The ground stubbornly damp. He carefully avoided the deeper puddles as he made his way down the streets.

It was difficult to navigate the only slightly familiar city streets, only becoming more complicated and less familiar as he reached denser buildings. Aelfraed glanced down streets for familiar landmarks. Something that would tell him he was in the right area. Or at least give him something to follow to get back on track if he had gotten lost. Down one street surrounded by tall stone buildings he caught sight of the monument. That he knew, he couldn't not. His father would always point it out, talking about why it had been built. The tall plinthed statue was a good sign that he was on the right track. He knew pretty much where he was going from there. He wasn't far now from the markets and shops he was looking for. He headed down the long street and soon enough found them.

The wide street was lined with narrow shop fronted buildings pushed against each other, leaving only the occasional space for a gate between. The buildings stretched above the shops with compact apartments. The middle of the street was filled with stalls and people bustling between them. The stalls were stacked with produce and products of smaller traders not able to afford a shop. Everything from crops from someone's small plot to carefully carved ornaments. It was busy. People were clustered at every stall and others walked past in a flow of people. Shops had people going in and out as he passed. He moved through the crowd, the noise drowning out his thoughts.

The Bakery was the first stop if he wanted to make sure he got the bread Caoimhe needed, still it wasn't as busy as it would have been earlier that morning. The shelves stood only half full or less of baked goods. The smell of bread was like a wall that hit him as he entered, along with a soft warmth that was pleasant after the brisk cold of the outside air.

"Hey! With you in a minute or whatever. Shout up if you need anything," the man at the counter called as a greeting. His head craned for a moment past the taller dark haired man he was currently serving.

He had rough cut dark brown hair. His Baker's uniform marked with remains of flour and the odd splodge of faded colour. There was a sort of second glance as Aelfraed nodded, however he turned his attention back to the other man at the counter who already had bags of shopping piled up at his feet.

Aelfraed glanced over the shelves and received a short nod from another similar looking man that was busy rearranging the still occupied trays while gathering up the empty ones for the afternoon restock. He was a bit taller than the other worker. His hair a little lighter. Yet their faces features were distinctly similar. The same nose. Both with wide thin mouths and squared jaws. He gave him another glance this one with brows more furrowed before flitting back into the back with his now empty tray. He couldn't help but wonder why they'd both looked at him like that. Did he really look as stressed as he felt?

Aelfraed couldn't help but focus on the tense raised voices that were coming from the back room. The indistinct shouts that made him flinch. He couldn't hear exactly what was being said but it left an uncomfortable tension in his body. The longer he listened as he moved round the shelves of the Bakery looking for the items from the list the more clear the shouting became.

"Hey the oven…!"

"It's too hot, are you trying to burn it!"

The other man slipped into the back. "We need more buns," he called as he stepped through the door.

"Get that flour out the pantry, we're going to need more than that!"

"It's burning!"

A loaf, a couple of pastries and half a dozen fruit scones. He scanned the list making sure he had everything needed from the Bakery. Sooner he was out the better. He leant down to add another half dozen plain scones to the bag. Someone else shuffled around him stacking shelves with even more fresh baked goods.

"Oh good morning we weren't expecting to see you today. How are you?" A voice came from beside him, there was a long pause. "Are you alright, Aethelric?"

Aelfraed stood suddenly, had his brother left work? Gotten off early, or had something gone wrong. He straightened up. The shop was mostly empty, the only new face was a short woman stood beside him. Her hair was a deep brown that looked almost black and was tied up into a tight bun held by a net.

Her dark eyes widened as she looked up at him, she quickly looked to the floor. "Ah sorry... I thought you were someone else."

She had thought he was Aethelric. He couldn't help but laugh. That hadn't happened in years. Not since his last growth spurt where he had passed Aethelric's height to the point that it was obvious. Yet leaning down and from behind those differences disappeared. She shifted awkwardly, comfortable by the probably embarrassing mix up.

"Sorry... I should just..." she started.

"Ah its fine, don't worry. I just wasn't expecting it. It's been a while," he reassured.

"A while?" She frowned thoughtfully, "You do look like Aethelric... oh wait! Are you his brother?"

He smiled and nodded, "We used to get mixed up all the time."

She chuckled herself, "That makes it a little less embarrassing. So what brings you to Newcastle, I think Aethelric said you were living in Edinburgh. Are you visiting him?" She asked as she continued stacking shelves with the breads that she had brought through.

"I just needed a break, thought I'd visit," he kept it simple, he didn't want to get into it with a stranger.

"You're lucky to be able to just Step to another city for a visit," she started wistfully, "My partner and I are currently saving to Step all the way to Bhārat to visit my grandparents."

He winced at the thought of such a long Step. The disorientation, the shift of time across the continent and into the next. The energy cost if they didn't have enough funds. He would despise it; he'd rather take a ship or at least have a good length of time to recover after the Step. At that distance many agreed if they had the time for the ship.

There was a crash and a loud bellow. Then the back door slammed open, Aelfraed flinched. The woman's head whipped round. A tall man with more bulk than the others and most definitely taller stormed out. His dark hair was dusted with flour and his brow was furrowed. He stomped over to the coat stand by the door.

The woman took an uncertain step forward. "Drust what happened?"

"Ask Stirgsen, apparently I don't know anything after all," he snapped as another older middle aged man followed through from the back. The man had a frustrated frown on his face.

"Messed up again Drust?" There was something nasty in the tone of the young man at the counter.

"Back off Caron before I…" He growled, throwing on a coat over his Baker's shirt.

"Drust," the middle aged man cut off with a stern tone, "cool off before you come back."

"Like I'm coming back," Drust scowled and slammed the door behind him rattling the glass.

The Baker sighed, a hand over his face, "Caron can you not rile him up so much."

"Why, why do you even put up with him? You've threatened my job for less when I was starting out."

He scowled, "that's my business and his. Nira could I get your help in the back until Drust comes back? I know it's meant to be your break soon but could you?"

"Would be better if he didn't," Caron muttered.

"Of course," Nira said quickly. She gave Aelfraed a little smile and a wave before heading off into the back, "hope you get the break you needed."

The Baker headed back soon after and Aelfraed couldn't help but listen as he found his last few things. A not quite silence that eased his worries. He took a calming breath and stepped over to the counter.

"Sorry about that, Drust can be such an ass."

"Ah no it's fine," he brushed it off as he handed over the right amount of coins.

There was thankfully no sign of the storming man by the time Aelfraed stepped back outside to continue his shopping. He didn't think anything would happen but his nerves were very much on edge. He slipped back into the crowd and ended up spending another hour or so wandering round including a pause to find some quick lunch before he started to head back up the street.

Chapter Four

There was a greater crowd as he passed by the Bakery again, the afternoon rush appeared to have come early and the crowd clustered round the shop waiting for space to get in. Stagnant and unmoving, they must have been struggling to keep up inside. The air buzzed with muttering. He skirted round the edge not wanting to have to cross the dense crowd that reached to the market tables in the centre of the street. Stall holders standing on their toes trying to see above the heads. As he walked he couldn't help but catch snippets of voices, voices that made him slow.

"It looked bad..." someone whispered to another, their voice breathy and broken.

Alfraed wondered what they were talking about, had the batch of bread been burnt? Had the angry storm out earlier been the result of a failed batch. That didn't seem right.

"Did someone summon a physician?" someone else called out louder. Aelfraed tried to stand taller to get a look over the crowd but couldn't see much more than the top of the shop windows. There was a building concern.

"I don't know…" was one response and the others were not much better. It was even more concerning to hear.

"It looked like sunburn…" someone else said, had an apprentice burned themselves; he had stopped entirely at this point.

"If the sun was inches from his face…" another responded with a horrified yet sarcastic snort.

There was still no sign of a physician, the street too quiet beyond the crowd. Something needed to be done, he needed to do something. It sounded potentially fatally bad if there wasn't help soon. He couldn't do much but he could try to do something, right? He heard nothing more as he pushed through the crowd as fast as it would let him. The door stood open but no one had gone through, he feared the ward might be up. That he wouldn't be able to get in anyway. He stumbled through with no resistance to an oppressive heat. The air rippled with a heated haze that distorted his vision. There was a distinct burnt smell in the air. It clung to his nose and made him cough. His arrival drew the attention of frantic apprentices, a bit of hope on their heat-reddened faces. The hope that Aelfraed was the physician they were waiting for, he wasn't. They would be disappointed. He could only hope to be of help.

On the floor between the apprentices was a body in what remained of white Baker's jacket. The same one he had seen on the Baker earlier. His skin was red and blackened with burns, blisters warping the shape. Almost unrecognisable as the man he had seen only hours earlier. Aelfraed felt his breathing grow faster, bringing in more rough hot air. He was shaking. The runes stitched onto the cuffs of the man's jacket that should have protected him had burned away, leaving tattered edges. Burnt all the way up to the ragged remains at his shoulders. The burned off white cloth hung heavy with water that pooled beneath. Burnt holes dotting the body of the shirt and his trousers. Aelfraed was frozen, his mind rattling along rails of uncomfortable distressing memories. The stillness, she hadn't been breathing either. Then he saw the man's chest rise, it hitched weakly. It was like he had been shaken to his senses. His mind still reeled as he hastily crossed the room, sloshing through pooled water. The man wasn't dead yet.

The door to the back room swung open with a forceful kick as Drust unexpectedly barrelled out with a bucket in hand. His dark hair was slick with sweat and had been roughly swept aside to keep the fringe out of his eyes. Water sloshed over the side of the bucket as he froze looking at Aelfraed. It was for less than a minute before he staggered forward the rest of the way, dumping the water over the burned man. The water flowed over the floor in flour clouded ripples. Aelfraed dropped to his knees in front of the Mr Stirgsen. Warm water soaked his trousers. The warm room had already rendered the fresh water useless in cooling the man any further. His raspy breaths drew Aelfraed's focus, unsteady. Aelfraed's hands shook, there wasn't much he could do to help. The first spell that came to mind was quickly discarded, too weak to be of any help. Something like this required something stronger, something more complex. Another came to mind. It was stronger, true but not the strongest. Still not as strong as was really needed. It would be enough for now. It had to be, he didn't have time to stumble through something more unfamiliar and didn't have a book to hand to recite from. He placed his hands on Mr Stirgsen's hot skin and grimaced at the feeling of his skin tingling. He knew this had to hurt. However he couldn't heal and handle the pain at the same time, not with any spell he knew well enough. A deep breath and then Aelfraed started to recite. It took a moment to get the rhythm. He thought through the process, how the skin would heal, how beneath it would do the same. He tried not to think how this spell was not for this intensity of damage. It would hopefully be enough to keep the man alive until help arrived. He kept going as the apprentices around him fell back into what they were doing. Water would splash over his hands at regular intervals. Warm air would move as they used trays to fan Mr Stirgsen, hoping the air would cool him. Despite the heat he could feel the cool tingle of the spell in his hands.

⁎

Aelfraed wasn't sure how long it had been, lost in his focus it felt both like hours and like minutes. Splashing footsteps moved swiftly behind him through the water, a woman appeared at his side. She wore a simple dark green apron over tan flared skirt like trousers and her hair plaited in a ring round her head with not a single hair out of place. Beside her she set down a satchel, the water repelled from it and her apron. She took a deep breath, settling out her heavy breathing, likely from having to run from the nearest Rune Step. It wouldn't have been far but at full pelt, it would still be quite a run. She quickly riffled through her bag, glass clinking lightly off glass.

"Keep that up a moment," she instructed before looking at the apprentices. "We need more water. You," she pointed to Caron

"Drust is..." He started.

"Doesn't matter. We need more. Colder the better, mopping him with the water off the floor is only going to make things worse. Ice cold if you can manage it," she insisted, Caron nodded before heading off into the back.

"Sh... should I go too?" asked Nira who had been fanning Stirgsen with a tray taken from a shelf. Trying to get the air in the room moving. Her voice wasn't the only thing to waver. Her face was flushed and had a sheen of sweat. She seemed to sway. Aelfraed for a moment thought it was just the heat rippling in the air but no.

The woman narrowed her eyes, looking Nira up and down. "No, take the rune diagram from my bag. Take it outside and copy it, I'll need it to get him to the Hall," she instructed, Aelfraed assumed that she too had spotted the unsteady way she stood.

She glanced at Brynn, "go with her, try to get rid of that crowd. I need to focus."

With Brynn shouting outside it was harder for Aelfraed to focus, his attention pulled more to the shouting than the faint whispers. The physician seemed to barely notice it, he had a feeling she just didn't want Nira out there alone if she was faint. Though Brynn probably needed a break from the heat too, none of them looked too good. Aelfraed had been there for a fraction of the time they had and already he was struggling. Breaths were sharp on his throat and his head swam a little.

The Physician pulled out of her satchel a jar, filled with pale blue almost water like liquid. She applied it to her hands, it clung like it was frozen yet warped downwards like icicles but never dripped. Aelfraed could tell she was about to use a more advanced spell. With a reagent like that it was hard to get more complex while still being portable and fast.

She looked at Aelfraed as she held her hands over the Baker's skin. "I'll handle the burns, do what you can for the pain."

Aelfraed nodded, he could definitely do something for the pain. Soothing pain without reagents was far simpler than repairing burns. He didn't need to think about how things went together, how it would heal. Instead distracting, numbing and disrupting the sensation reaching the brain. He still had to focus. Focus on the feeling of cold. On how the nerves and receptors threaded through the body, how to block them. Which ones were even safe to block without causing more harm.

Aelfraed broke his chant the moment she started hers, he cleared his dry throat. He tried not to let the way his head felt in the stuffy heat get to him and then began again with a new spell. The rhythm was softer, calmer. It was a far more familiar spell to him, he had used it many times and even before that it had been used on him. If Mr Stirgsen had been conscious it would have pulled his attention away, as he wasn't there was no visible change from his spell, he remembered what it felt like though.

The lack of focus as his mind drifted, gaze wandering over shelves of his father's study.

The words on the books were like a dream, readable in the moment and yet he couldn't remember them from looking from one book to the next. He had only remembered the broken bone in his arm existed in the aftermath, looking back he was sure the spell was rather extreme for the situation.

His chanting mingled with that of the Physician's, the ointment on her hands glowing softly. Where it touched it would soak in, blistering red shedding layers as fresh healthy skin formed beneath. The skin was raw and red scarred. She focused on the worst and most vital areas. Drust and Caron would come back and forth with water. Careful as they poured the water not to catch her hands. Soon her hands were bare of the ointment. Mr Stirgsen's skin was still red, in many places still blackened and burned. She had done as much as she could here.

Her chanting flowed elegantly from spell to words. "Help me get him out to the Step," and then back into chanting, this time matching him. Syncing up and pulling out of her bag with a spare hand a folded cloth trimmed with runes.

She handed the cloth to Aelfraed before gently shifting Stirgsen to allow Aelfraed to unfold the cloth and position it under him. The water was pushed away from it once it was fully stretched out under him.

Aelfraed lifted one end of the cloth and the Physician the other. For a moment as he lifted he could feel the weight of the man before the runes activated and then he was light. Light enough that they could carry him out to the street with little jostling of his injuries. While the man was light, the wet floor still made navigating the Bakery difficult. His foot would slip and he would have to snap out a few words that would for a moment freeze his foot to the floor.

Outside the street almost seemed quiet, a stillness in comparison to the chaos of what had happened. The pair that had been sent out were leaning against the wall, resting in the cool fresh air. Aelfraed found himself shivering in his sweat and water soaked clothes, where only earlier that day he hadn't. They set Mr Stirgsen down on the rune circle that had been scrawled on the stone path with charcoal. Its lines had been redrawn a couple of times, the faint signs of more wobbly lines still remained. It held a series of runes that he assumed related to where in the city the hospital was and a sharp pointed kite shape pointing in the direction. The Physician stepped into the circle, she gave it a quick glance over. Bending over with charcoal in hand to correct something before her spell shifted again. They both vanished in the flash and a whoosh of air. Charcoal burning away.

Aelfraed blinked away the distortions from his eyes and felt the oncoming faintness of overheating. The adrenaline was wearing off as he slumped down next to the apprentices against the wall. The other two soon joined them, more layers were shed despite the cold. Heavy breaths broken with sobs and muttered curse words as what happened sank in.

Chapter Five

Before the cold became unpleasant there was another bright flare, Aelfraed and the apprentices beside him began stumbling to their feet. They all knew that meant the City Wardens were there. The two men stood before them in matching gambesons, the padded patches were littered with embroidered runes. Protection of various kinds. Alternating black and blue and the embroidery in a light silvery grey without the sparkle of actual silver thread. From their belts hung an assortment of tools. Their issued focus; a rod of dark metal engraved with spirals filled with brass. They were less effective than a custom one but easier to mass produce. They also carried metal bands engraved with runes, a rune pad, and pouches of various other things. The taller of the two Wardens glared with an imposing scowl, the shape of his grey peppered beard only made the scowl deeper. Aelfraed couldn't help but be reminded of his father's own short temper.

"Alright, I want to know what happened here, and I want to know now!" he snapped, Aelfraed shrunk a little at the demand he didn't really know the answer to. Not in a way that could satisfy the question.

Brynn glanced at the others, his gaze lingered on the more shaken members of the group. He stepped forward to take charge. "I was in the back working on the next batch of loaves, I heard Nira scream," he paused for a calming breath trying not to crack at the memory. "Rushed in, I thought she had just dropped a tray or something but then I saw Stirgsen, he was lying on the floor... he was so burned it looked like... I thought..."

"And then what did you do? Because you definitely didn't summon the Wardens," the Warden scolded, "who knows how far the assailant has gotten in the time it took for the Physician to report it."

Brynn shuffled his feet and glanced away, "I..."

"I'm sorry, we were a little busy... you know, trying to save Stirgsen's life," Drust bit back.

The Warden looked him up and down, his brows raised in an incredulous manner, "as honourable as that is there are fou... five even," he corrected, his eyes landing on Aelfraed, "mot one of you got a moment? Who was it that even summoned the Physician?"

"I did Sir, it was just after Drust came back," Brynn said, gesturing to Drust behind him.

"Wardens O'Darachir and Wynnstan, skip the sir," O'Darachir said quickly before asking, "came back?"

"Yeah…"

Drust cut Brynn before he could continue, "I'd stepped out for a bit before we closed up. Got back to find Stirgsen on the floor."

"Can you show us where this was?" Warden Wynnstan asked.

It drew Aelfraed's attention momentarily from his focus on Warden O'Darachir. The other Warden was a shorter man with curly red hair that was cut short. He was distinctly less intimidating if only because the man couldn't be compared to the scowling face of his father.

Drust nodded and led the way. They filed back into the Bakery, Wardens following behind. The wall of stuffy heat hit Aelfraed all over again, he caught sight of the others grimacing as they walked into the heat. The younger of the Wardens recoiled slightly. The air was still strong with the smell of burning; the trail of smoke from the back curling through the door was new. Something else was burning. Brynn scrambled for the back room, the Wardens grabbed for him and started reaching for their belts. He returned before they made it to the door with a tray of small loaves that were burnt black.

"Sorry… I thought it best to deal with that," he said, setting the tray down and stepping round the Wardens to stand next to his brother. "Last thing we need now is a fire," the apprentices stood awkwardly by the door, uncomfortable being back in the Bakery.

"You probably should have said something," Wynnstan said.

"Any other safety concerns that need dealing with?" O'Darachir said with a scowl.

"Ah no, sorry."

Aelfraed watched Warden O'Darachir warily as he sloshed through the layer of water, "I take it Stirgsen was found here?" They nodded, "Wynnstan you deal with the witnesses, I'm going to take a look around first. Get the full picture of the place."

Warden Wynnstan nodded hastily. He rummaged through a pocket on his belt till he found a notebook and fountain pen. He looked at them, "right… so you said you were in the back and you were out, um was there anyone else here?"

Warden O'Darachir crouched down to examine the wet floor where the Baker had been.

"No... just us. We'd closed up to restock," Caron said.

"Oh? Who and what's he doing here then?" O'Darachir asked, glancing over from the other side of the room. Wynnstan was doing the questioning but he was listening.

"Ah um Aelfraed Agmundrson, just a passer-by, I just saw something was happening and saw fit to assist," he explained uncomfortable under the Warden's gaze.

"He helped heal Stirgsen," Nira spoke up.

"Oh... a physician? Shouldn't you be with Physician Caldwell?" Wynnstan questioned.

"Oh no... I'm not... I'm still a student... I just helped it was really more um, physician Caldwell you said right?" He corrected sheepishly, he felt awkward. He hadn't really done much, if anything at all really. His spell had barely any effect. His father would have been more useful.

"Still did something, lucky you were here really," Wynnstan said with a smile, O'Darachir eyed Aelfraed with a thoughtful look on his face.

"Honestly I was lucky the ward was down otherwise I wouldn't have even been able to get in," Aelfraed said, he didn't really feel all that lucky but that had to have been some sort of luck. Luck that someone had forgotten about it when they closed up. Maybe more Stirgsen's luck than his own.

"The ward was down?" Wynnstan questioned.

"Drust probably left it open in his rush to get water," Caron said dismissively.

"No, I came in the back."

"Ah actually Caron, I opened it, wanted to let in some air and removed the ward so that the Physician could get in," Brynn corrected.

"I see, Nira?" the Warden turned to the girl, "he said that you had found Stirgsen, what did you see?"

She gave a slightly frowning glance to Brynn who nodded with an encouraging smile, "right, he was just lying there, I was bringing through some of the next batch from the back while Brynn watched the ovens. I... I thought he was dead," her voice shook as she spoke, "he had been fine... I'd only been gone... 15 minutes? Maybe?"

"Where were the rest of you? Anyone see anything?" Wynnstan asked.

"We didn't see anything, I was in the back manning the ovens like she said till Nira screamed. Caron was in the yard," Brynn said, indicating to his brother.

"15 minutes isn't long, with the ward up that leaves one of you," O'Darachir said, coming back over, "there is no sign of forced entry, the only way back in is with a keystone," he said looking at Drust.

The Warden was right that 15 minutes by Nira's estimate didn't leave a lot of time for that level of heat to be generated, especially to the extent to not only heat the room but crack tiles and burn away the protection runes on the Baker's uniform. Not the strongest fire protection runes but should have been able to handle the temperatures normally expected in a Bakery. It would have had to have been a far more powerful elemental spell than any baker's apprentice needed to know.

"What was that?" O'Darachir questioned with brows raised, eyes on Aelfraed who was only just beginning to realise he had been thinking aloud or at least mumbling about it to himself, "you said something about protection runes?

"Was it really that hot in here?" Wynnstan squeaked as they pulled at the collar of their gambeson, probably longing to take it off.

"Ah sorry I didn't mean to interrupt, I was just thinking aloud," Aelfraed said quickly, brushing it off. Hoping the man would just move on.

"While I appreciate the apology, what you were thinking is relevant so if you would..." O'Darachir pushed.

"Yes... of course," he stumbled over the unexpected request and acceptance of the apology. The kind his father would never have given for the interruption, "I don't know how bad it was when Nira arrived but when I got here the shop was almost unbearably hot. The tiles around where the Baker was are broken, I don't think they were earlier but the runes on his uniform, those definitely were from the heat. They were burnt away completely and even after that he burned so badly. I doubt that baker's apprentices learn elemental spells of that strength," he tried not to ramble.

O'Darachir glanced back over to the broken tiles on the floor, heat shattered, "not the sort of spell that would belong in a Bakery."

"Not unless they wanted to incinerate the bread," Wynnstan frowned, he looked towards the shelves that were cracked and the blackened bread on them. They looked as bad as the bread left in the oven too long.

"What about someone who's been apprenticed to a smith?" Caron said with some venom, shooting a glare at Drust.

"You insinuating something you little…" Drust growled, a fist clenching. Aelfraed flinched away despite not being the target.

"What that you attacked Stirgsen? Yeah! You're the only one who could have cast that spell, we all know you hated him!" he shouted.

"Caron," Brynn started as Drust lunged.

O'Darachir grabbed Drust by the wrist, only a little away from Caron's face. "That's enough of that!" he stated firmly. "While that is an interesting accusation I would rather have some solid evidence. Care to explain that statement?"

Drust scowled, pulling his hand out of the Warden's grip. "I used to be apprenticed to a smith, that's it."

"Bull, we all know you didn't get along. Even he saw it today," Caron said, pointing to Aelfraed.

"Caron I'm sure that wasn't enough for Drust to…" Nira glanced at Drust.

"Something happened between you and Stirgsen today?" Wynnstan asked. "What happened?"

"It was nothing, I just left to get more stuff from the warehouse," Drust stated.

"I'm sorry but you did leave with some… force. I don't know what happened but you didn't look… happy," Aelfraed commented, his wording careful. He eyed the man's fists.

"Why'd you even bother coming back? Very short never," Caron scoffed.

"Why do you care?" Drust scowled.

"Want to elaborate on what that argument was about?" O'Darachir raised his brows questioningly.

"Ugh fine, yes me and the old man argued. A lot even but I wouldn't try to off him," Drust defended with a glare.

"Argued about what?" Wynnstan asked, taking notes in his book.

"Those two, all sorts. Drust is always burning the bread," Caron said.

"Caron, enough. Drust is still learning," his older brother cut him off. "I'm sorry Wardens, Drust and Stirgsen had issues. Drust's hard headed and Stirgsen strict. It added up."

Drust mumbled about not being hard headed under his breath but didn't protest the statements loudly, "doesn't matter, I didn't do it."

"Still learning? He's been here months! In that time Stirgsen threatened my job five times when I was new. It doesn't take Rune Step Engineer to spot the favourite!" Caron complained loudly.

"Bit odd to have the apprentice you have issues with as the favourite. Why were you the favourite?" Warden Wynnstan asked.

"I'm not, Stirgsen expected me to keep up with everyone else," Drust insisted.

"But he didn't fire you when you couldn't, why?" Wynnstan pushed.

"Like I know," he shrugged, "maybe he liked watching me struggle."

"He didn't, he wouldn't do that," Nira shakily smiled at Drust, "he knew you needed the work."

"Yeah right, I doubt that," Drust rolled his eyes.

"Is that the sort of man Mr Stirgsen is?" Wynnstan asked.

Nira nodded, "he's always looking out for others even if he does run a tight ship."

"Pft that just the favouritism talking. You weren't far behind Drust," Caron scoffed.

"Fine, enough. Clearly you all have different opinions of the sort of man he is. Right now we need find out what happened," O'Darachir cut off the argument before it could start up again, "for now I think it best you show me where the rest of you were when Stirgsen was found."

"Right, through here Wardens," Brynn led them through to the back, everyone else following behind.

**

The room was only a little smaller than the shop itself or maybe that was just how cramped the space was with all of them crammed in there. Benches filled the middle of the room and various parts of the walls. A few trays of unbaked bread stood abandoned near the ovens that were still pumping out heat. A dusting of flour coated every surface including the floor, where there was a line of trodden damp floor from the trips for water. The room was still warm but cooler than the shop.

"I was in here and Caron was out the back," Brynn said, indicating to the door set in the back wall. Through its windows a small yard could be seen.

O'Darachir walked over kicking up more flour, it opened easily. No ward and no lock as he stuck out his head. Glanced in both directions before turning back to the group.

"You said you opened the door, correct?" he said looking at Brynn who nodded. He then looked to Drust, "and you came in the back? Did you run into Caron at any point?"

"No, he was already in the room with Stirgsen," Drust replied.

"I wasn't far behind Brynn, saw him run off through the window," Caron explained.

"Wynnstan, note that there is a back gate. Any of them could have slipped round," O'Darachir commented, closing the door.

"Any of us?" Caron looked offended. "If anyone had come past I would have seen."

"That may be true but is there anyone that can confirm that you were in the yard the whole time? Anyone that can confirm that your brother was in here the whole time and that you are not just covering for each other. As I have said, I would prefer tangible evidence to the hearsay of who saw who," O'Darachir explained, arms folded in front of him, "it wouldn't be the first time someone's lied to me. Not by a long shot."

"What about that door? Where does that go?" Wynnstan asked, pointing to a door in the other wall.

"Oh that's the pantry. Just storage basically. No one in there could have gotten round the front without fancy stuff with runes," Drust chuckled a little, "see?"

He opened the pantry door, a few steps led down and faded out into a dark unlit basement room. Aelfraed leaned closer to see if he could spot anything but even as his eyes adjusted to the dark all he could spot was shelving in the small space. There was something lying on the floor in a heap, light coloured and definitely fabric.

"What is that?" Aelfraed asked, squinting at it, trying to get a better look through the dark without going in.

"Hmmm Wynnstan? Would you?" O'Darachir asked, turning to him.

"Yes, give me a second," he responded quickly muttering another word to bring a light to his hand before hopping down the stairs.

Chapter Six

It was a baker's over shirt, like the ones the apprentices had all long since shed. Shed before Aelfraed had even arrived. Similar to the Baker's damaged one they held a lot of protection but sometimes in the heat it was still best removed. Wynnstan picked it up with the barest tips of his fingers not wanting to touch too much of it. It hung from his fingers, surprisingly dry as he headed back up. It must have been before the water got involved. O'Darachir grabbed a sleeve to take a closer look at the runes, burned through like the Baker's. Aelfraed couldn't help the frown on his face. He gave a cautious glance around him. He had still been hoping that there was an outsider involved. He hadn't wanted to think that someone close would do it, even with the arguments. Maybe, just maybe there still was a chance of that. Maybe this was Nira's shirt. Strange for it to be down there but first on the scene she would have taken the worst of the heat.

"Is that Nira's?" Brynn asked.

Nira frowned at him and shook her head, "it's not mine... I left mine in the front."

O'Darachir took the shirt. "Wynnstan, see if you can find the rest of these," The man nodded and ran off into the front. "Mr Agmundrson? You are a fairly impartial individual here. What do you know about rune overload... you did mention the runes before."

Aelfraed twitched a little at the use of his last-name but nodded. "I know some," he said, reaching out and waiting for the man to nod before lifting the other sleeve. "I assume you are more interested in a comparison to Stirgsen's runes than the technical side of things."

O'Darachir frowned. "I know what I need to know about how it works, a comparison will do."

"Right, sorry," Aelfraed looked away to focus on the shirt, a little embarrassed. Of course the Warden knew how an overload worked. The set amount of strain the threads or material could take before they would be spent. At least he hadn't just rambled on without asking.

He looked over the sleeve, thinking back to what he had seen. Trying to focus only on the memory of the Baker's sleeves and not the horrid burns underneath. The way the sleeves were practically non-existent, the same way as this shirt cuff were. He frowned, the sleeves were burnt through, where scraps of the cuffs remained the tattered shapes no longer resembled the runes they had once been.

"Warden O'Darachir, if someone were wearing this shirt they would have to be burnt badly, not as bad as Stirgsen but still bad unless they got out awfully fast. Even then they would be burnt," Aelfraed said looking up from the shirt.

He glanced down at his own red hands, not burnt but a little scalded from the heat of Mr Stirgsen's body. It blended a little with his arm where he was red from the heightened heat of the Bakery. He had no doubt that some of the apprentices likely had it worse but none had complained of burns. If they'd been wearing that shirt they would have burned even if they had been fast. Surely he would have noticed that at least after the chaos.

"Hands, all of you now," O'Darachir demanded.

The apprentices each showed their hands with little hesitation. Their hands were in varied states of scalded red. Drust's were similar to his own. While the other three were worse. Nira and Caron were blistered alongside the raw red. Nira's were the worst but that made sense for her extended time exposed. O'Darachir frowned.

Wynnstan returned with an arm full of shirts a moment later, "I found three out there."

The shirts were laid out on a nearby bench; the flour on the bench didn't matter much with how much was already caked into the shirts. The three were in various states, one worse than the others. From the sizes it was clear that the one from the pantry was Drust's. A tall but narrow one was probably Brynn's. Two smaller shirts were laid out next to it that would have been Nira's and Caron's. One of the smaller ones was the worst. The runes on it almost burned up, leaving little holes cut out in their shape the edges burnt brown. The brown was in patches further up as if the sleeve had caught a bit once the rune's protection was weakened. The other two were mottled with brown around the runes with the odd hole burnt through.

O'Darachir gave Drust a pointed look. "Loose something in there on your way in?"

"What? No, I didn't even have my shirt on before all this!" Drust snapped back, he stared at the shirt. "Someone else must have taken it."

"Are you sure about that? We now have motive, opportunity and physical evidence. It isn't looking good for you," O'Darachir said as he reached for the metal bands at his waist. "Blast Stirgsen, then hop round the back and throw the shirt in the pantry on the way."

"Seriously? It can't have been me! I didn't have it on when I left! Brynn you saw me," Brynn shook his head, "argh fine, Nira?"

Nira looked at Brynn for a moment, "I... I saw him. He wasn't wearing it."

O'Darachir groaned with frustration that was clear on his frowning face, "great, anyone able to second that?"

Nira looked to Caron and Aelfraed, "you saw him too right?"

"I didn't notice. Figured he'd be wearing it though. It's not exactly warm out," Caron said.

Aelfraed frowned, he couldn't remember. He had been too distracted by the shouting to notice. He didn't have an answer but there was something else. Something that was nagging at him; bothering him, "I can't remember sorry," he apologised.

What was it? Aelfraed thought hard. Trying and failing to block out the angry shouts of Drust as he defended himself, struggling against the grip of the Wardens. Each shout had him flinch, interrupting his thoughts. Something was missing. Something he couldn't quite put his finger on. He couldn't help but think about how Nira kept looking at Brynn, the way she would frown. The way she would look before and after either said anything. Had she been covering for him? No she was saying things against him, or against his word. So what was it?

The shouting moved away as the Wardens pulled Drust through into the shop. Brynn moved to follow them and as he passed Nira she pulled away from the attempted comforting hand aiming for her shoulder.

Something wasn't right, "are you okay?" Aelfraed asked stepping closer to Nira.

"…yes… just shaken…" she said with a deep breath.

"It's more than that, did Brynn do something?" Aelfraed asked.

"I just... don't know what to think...I don't know what to do... he... I... I wasn't wrong," she ended firmly.

"Wrong? About the shirt?" He asked. That was it. Something about the shirts was wrong. Did he remember seeing Drust without? No he still couldn't remember.

She looked up at him. "I don't... I don't know why he's lying. Maybe not about seeing Drust but... but he never went near the door."

Aelfraed frowned. Why, why lie. That meant the door had been left open. Intentionally? Why hide that unless blame was meant to fall on someone already inside but Brynn hadn't covered Drust with the shirt so who was he protecting? Maybe it was a mistake, just a misunderstanding but maybe it wasn't. Add that to his own uncertainty about the shirts. That feeling that something was wrong. If they were right then they needed to say something. If they were wrong what was the harm of being sure.

"That's odd. Maybe it's just a mistake but it might not be. Best if we bring it up to the Wardens. Better wrong than sorry," it wasn't a philosophy that his father would have agreed with but O'Darachir seemed like the type to listen to their concerns.

"I don't want to think he did it... but I don't want to think Drust would do it either," she said.

"Even more reason to say something, if we're right then Drust is taking the fall," Aelfraed pushed, "Let's catch them before they leave."

He could still hear the struggle through the shop. He had tried to block out the shouts and the clatter of trays. He hadn't been able to block out Drust's shouting, insisting his innocence. Nira nodded.

**

They quickly headed through into the shop. Water still sloshing round their feet. The Wardens were wrestling a bit with Drust near the door.

"Sorry to interrupt again but... well Nira and I have some concerns. We don't think it was Drust," Aelfraed said, his voice rising to get the attention of the Wardens. Nira shifted beside him, her eyes on Brynn.

O'Darachir paused and looked back at them with a frown, "concerns? Look unless these concerns are evidence, then you best leave it for the courts."

Aelfraed looked to Nira, she was shaking a little. Some of her confidence lost with Brynn watching her. Her hands clenched as she took a deep breath. "… I don't… I don't know if it helps… but Brynn. Brynn's been lying. He… he didn't go near the door."

Drust stopped struggling, his eyes finding Brynn. He glared with a furrowed brow, "see he's a liar! It wasn't me! I wasn't wearing the shirt!"

"Did you lie?" O'Darachir asked.

"I didn't," Brynn insisted.

"Are you sure about that? The one person that saw you now says you didn't and Drust would have had to still move pretty fast to not end up just as charred as Mr Stirgsen. Is that really enough time to close the door and reseal the ward before Nira returned?" O'Darachir said tracing back through the chain of events.

"I didn't lie, why would I? Drust is just someone I work with. I opened the door, Nira must have just been distracted with Stirgsen," Brynn defended.

"Screw you!" Drust shouted pulling against Wynnstan's grip.

"You were pretty distracted, even I saw him," Caron commented.

That didn't make sense; that was wrong. "Didn't you think Drust opened it when he came back?" Aelfraed asked.

"He... he did say that and he wasn't in until just before Drust," Nira said.

"I..." Caron started his eyes wide and glancing to Brynn.

"Oh, didn't you say you ran in after seeing Brynn run, through the window out back?" Wynnstan asked, letting go of the now not struggling Drust to flick through his notebook. "What took you so long?"

"What does it even matter, Drust is the only one capable of casting that spell anyway. Rest of us wouldn't know where to start," Caron snapped.

"Yeah I could have done it but I'm not stupid enough to only use a bloody baker's shirt as protection against a spell meant to melt metal!" Drust bit back. "One of you idiots is lucky to be alive and I think I'm looking at him!"

"It was your shirt!" Caron yelled.

Aelfraed paused. It was Drust's shirt, but that was what was wrong. Just Drust's shirt would have left him burned. Maybe not as bad as the Baker but he should have been burned. Yet the man had scalds the least of all of them. Bakers' runes couldn't hold up against that, they'd need more protection.

"More, how could they have gotten more?" Aelfraed mumbled to himself. There had to be a way, or they would have had two injured parties. They would need more runes.

Aelfraed frowned and whipped round bolting back into the back room.

"What's gotten into him?" he just caught Wynnstan saying.

****

Aelfraed's hands hit against the bench as he forced himself to a sudden stop. The flour on the floor making it almost as precarious as the water covered tiles of the shop. He snatched up the most burnt shirt. Looking over the arms, away from the burns. He was sure he had seen it. There, the mark. A faded old red brown stain almost lost in the browns of burnt fabric. A touch more red from some berry in the fruit scones, probably. Amongst all the burns it had looked like any other but it wasn't a burn. It wasn't Nira's shirt, it was Caron's. It didn't make sense for the last one in to have the worst condition to their runes, unless they were not last. With both shirts layered up then, then with enough speed someone could get out with only some scalding and the odd blister. Especially if there were other protection runes hidden under his clothes.

Wynnstan appeared in the doorway, "um Mr Agmundrson? What's wrong?"

Aelfraed glanced over, still holding the shirt, "it wasn't Drust. This shirt is Caron's, not Nira's, this mark. I saw it earlier. When I was first in the shop. If he was second to last then his shouldn't be the worst. He must have layered his shirt with Drust's bigger one to protect himself from burning. Drust wouldn't have been able to do that."

"Are you sure? It makes some sense, Drust's hands didn't seem very burnt at all," Wynnstan asked.

Aelfraed nodded, "I'm sure I saw it. Might even have more runes under his other shirt."

Wynnstan pulled back round the door, "O'Darachir, check under Caron's shirt. The worst one's his!"

*

Aelfraed rushed out after Wynnstan, to find O'Darachir and Drust grappling with Caron and Brynn.

"Let go! I didn't do anything!"

"Wynnstan says otherwise," O'Darachir stated completely trusting Wynnstan, "what am I looking for?" he asked as he yanked up Caron's shirt.

"More runes possibly. Either way Mr Agmundrson says the shirt was his. It would make sense if he layered them," Wynnstan explained.

"It wasn't me... I... I just don't like being hot," Caron protested as his vest was revealed, runes roughly embroidered across it with various holes where they had burnt up.

"A lot of damage for the second to last one in," O'Darachir levelled the man with a pointed look.

"I..."

"Enough, the evidence is rather stacked against you, both of you considering Brynn's attempts to cover it up," O'Darachir strapped a metal runed band around Caron's wrists that tightened to fit snuggly, "I wouldn't be surprised if Brynn used that burning bread as an opportunity to hide that shirt."

Brynn looked at the floor but didn't protest the accusation. Wynnstan strapped his band round Brynn's wrists taking the man from Drust's grip. Caron continued to struggle as he was dragged out.

"Thank you for speaking up and for the expertise," Wynnstan thanked Nira and Aelfraed before steering Brynn by the arms out into the street.

Aelfraed sagged, expertise. It felt rather over the top. He wasn't really an expert in anything. At least he had been able to help. He followed the remaining two apprentices outside into the cool air.

Nira dropped to the ground outside and sat there leaning against the wall. Aelfraed gathered his abandoned shopping that had been left by the door.

He looked over at them. "Are you two going to be okay?"

"Eventually..." Nira muttered. "Drust... I..."

"It's fine. At least you said something eventually," he said gruffly, he looked to Aelfraed. "Glad you figured something out or I'd be off with the Wardens."

"Ah... it was nothing... really. I'm sure it would have worked out."

"Unlikely, at that point my only other out was if Stirgsen recovered and that's even if he saw the brat," He frowned. "If he didn't, he'd probably think I'd done it too."

"I doubt he would have from the sounds of it," Aelfraed said.

Drust laughed awkwardly, "Seriously, does everyone think he didn't hate me but me?"

Nira smiled, "that's because he doesn't, hopefully you'll see that too when he wakes up."

"I'll believe it when I see it," Drust sighed.

"I still don't get why, was he really that angry. That jealous? I guess I didn't know them as well as I thought," Nira questioned looking up at them, "I thought you and Brynn were friends."

"Friends, ha, friendly terms at best. Figures they'd both throw me into the furnace to keep themselves out of trouble," Drust scowled.

Nira smiled at Aelfraed, "thank you for stepping in both times."

"Ah it was…"

"Say it was nothing again and I'll lose it," Drust snapped, "it definitely wasn't nothing."

Aelfraed sighed, "Okay…"

Aelfraed only lingered a little longer; he wanted to make sure that both were fine. Their scalded hands were easily soothed and the heat stroke that he too was feeling the early signs of was reduced. They'd all need some rest and a good amount of water to clear the rest. As for the mental there was little he could do there

Chapter Seven

He drifted slowly back through familiar streets, backtracking even through the disoriented diversions he had taken on the way to the market, in the hopes of not getting more lost. His head pounded in time with his steps only making it harder to remember if he had turned left or right. It was far later than he had expected to be heading back and the night was beginning to roll in. A dark blue cast to the sky. He knew he wasn't going to be back before Aethelric or Caoimhe. They'd think he'd gotten lost. Of course he had to manage to worry them over what should have been a simple errand.

Aelfraed was relieved to find himself coming out of a narrow walled path onto the right street before the dark had set in enough for the lamps to light. As he pushed the gate the door swung open. Aethelric stood there his jacket on as he was turned back to say something to Caoimhe who was stood in the hallway behind him.

He'd opened the door so quickly that Aelfraed was sure he had been about to go out looking for him. Caoimhe pointed and Aethelric's head whipped round. His eyes widened as they caught on Aelfraed.

"Aelfie, where were you? Did you really get that lost?" he tried to joke as he took off his coat. "Aren't you cold?"

Caoimhe slipped out past him over to Aelfraed, "come on, get in before you catch cold," she hurried him inside.

He sagged a little in the gentle warmth of the house, the light draft as she closed the door finally provoked a shiver from him.

"I wish I had just gotten lost," Aelfraed sighed, hanging up his unworn coat.

Aethelric gave him a worried look. "What happened? Father didn't manage to find you, did he?"

He paused, wouldn't that have been a blessing. Not that hours ago he would have even thought that. He'd face his father a million times over what had actually happened.

"No," He shook his head, "it wasn't him. There... there was an incident. Mr Stirgsen, the Baker, he was attacked."

Aethelric's eyes widened. "Is he alright? Are you alright? What about everyone else?" he looked Aelfraed over.

"I'm fine, just overheated... and shaken... bad memories. Don't know about Mr Stirgsen, he was alive at least last I saw. No one else was hurt," he cut himself off before he spiralled. He didn't want to talk about what happened.

He didn't want to have to tell Aethelric that someone he might have thought a friend would have attempted to murder another maybe friend. If Nira was a friend he no doubt knew the others at least. It was silly, he would find out eventually but Aelfraed just didn't want to be the one to break the news. Doing so would mean explaining what had gone on, which was something he didn't want to do. Not now.

"Alright, we'll keep an eye out in the paper. I'm sure he'll be okay. He's in good hands no doubt," Aethelric said with a light comforting smile.

**_{*}

The next morning didn't really happen for Aelfraed. He dragged himself down the stairs just a little after noon. His thoughts circling around the events of the day before and the dread of his father's inevitable appearance.

He found Aethelric on the stairs, heading up with a smile on his face. A smile that was more real than the shaky comforting ones of the day before. He was carrying the paper folded up under his arm while the other hand held the bannister of the narrow staircase.

"Ah Aelfie there you are, thought you might still be asleep," he said with a smile as he held out the paper, "looks like Mr Stirgsen should make a recovery, though I doubt he'll be running the shop anymore."

"That's good, could have been a lot worse..." Aelfraed said, trying not to think about how the man had looked.

Aelfraed took the paper and skimmed down the article. It wasn't very long but he was glad to see that Mr Stirgsen was expected to recover. He did however cringe at the sight of his own last name. He still didn't feel like he deserved that extra attention never mind just appearing as Mr Agmundrson as if he were his father. Even if he had helped surely it didn't warrant that.

"It definitely could have been, I'm planning to head over and see Nira after lunch. Make sure she's alright," Aethelric said, "come on, I'll throw together something for you too. You're probably hungry."

Aelfraed nodded without protest, following his brother down the stairs. He hung back in the kitchen listening to Aethelric talk about various things. How work was, what Caoimhe had been talking about that morning. He helped in the odd places he could but left the majority of the prep work to Aethelric. It wasn't that he didn't want to help more it was that he really didn't know his way around a kitchen. If he was to try it would likely result in something getting burnt.

It was while he stood there that he realised something. His name was in the paper. The paper he knew his father read every day even though he was in a different city. Looking for any reason to call for a visit. The appearance wasn't just inevitable it was imminent.

He considered just going back, before his father turned up. Maybe he would get there before he left if he braved the Rune Step. It wasn't fair to bring his problems and failings onto Aethelric's shoulders. This had all been a mistake. The whole trip. He should have just stayed and worked harder.

"Aelfie? What's wrong?" Aethelric asked two plates in hand as he looked at him with a concerned frown.

For a moment he considered lying and just heading back but it wasn't fair to leave Aethelric to face their father if he wasn't fast enough. He wouldn't be and it would just be another of his mistakes.

"Father reads the paper… he'll be on his way."

Chapter Eight

The day passed on edge, the looming appearance of their father kept Aelfraed from even considering relaxing. Apprehension had him pacing the hall. Every sound outside had him glancing to the door. Dreading the moment that his father would appear to berate him for his foolish choices. He deserved it but if he was the first seen then maybe Aethelric wouldn't be drawn into it.

Aethelric leant against the door frame to the drawing room, "Aelfie, please come sit down."

He paused, "I can't... I can't..." if he did then Aethelric would open the door.

"Aelfie, you need to relax. This isn't going to help," he insisted.

Aelfraed shook his head and continued his pacing. Aethelric sighed and then stiffened. Straightening up as if a loud noise had gone off beside him.

Aelfraed paused, "He's here isn't he."

Aethelric nodded and stepped slowly towards the door. Aelfraed followed after hoping to get in front of him but failing. Aethelric took a deep breath before opening it with a fake smile plastered onto his face.

Tension drained from both their shoulders at the sight of Caoimhe digging through her bag for her keystone as she stood on the doorstep.

She looked at both of them her brows raised in confusion, "what are you two doing?"

"Father's likely on his way. Aelfie's name ended up in the paper," Aethelric explained.

She frowned, "and? He's in Edinburgh why would he... he doesn't does he?" her tone taking on a touch of an angry growl.

"Apparently yes," Aethelric sighed.

"Great, just great. If he turns up on that step he's not coming in," she said with a finality that Aelfraed knew was futile. Their father didn't take no for an answer.

**

Aelfraed woke to a bellow crashing through his dreams, "Aelfraed! Get down here now!"

His eyes shot open this time for real after several scattered anxious dreams of what might happen. The shout turned into muffled loud voices not quite loud enough to reach him through the floor. Aelfraed frowned dragging himself out of bed, that was Aelthelric he could just about hear along with the angry raised tones of their father. He'd turned up while he slept and now Aethelric was taking the brunt of his ire. He couldn't let Aethelric take the blame for this. He would try, even if Aelfraed didn't deserve the help.

He slipped out of the bedroom and into the corridor, softly stepping down the narrow stairs to the landing overlooking the hallway. Their father stood at the bottom gripping the banister tightly, turned away to face Aethelric. He couldn't see his face but could imagine the deep scowl and crunched eyebrows along with the tinge of red to his skin.

Aethelric's own eyes were narrowed and focused on their father. Aelfraed wouldn't have been able to hold that glare. He stood closer to the door that still hung slightly open, forgotten in the argument. A cold draft curling through the corridor.

Caoimhe appeared ducking past Aethelric from the dining room. She shot their father a pointed glare as she swung the front door closed. It clattered off the frame with a bang but stuck and stayed closed.

"Don't try that with me Aethelric. I know he's here," his father demanded, folding his arms. Aelfraed stilled, half wanting to escape back up the stairs unnoticed.

"Fine okay, he's here but why are you?" Aethelric said pointedly, "he's allowed to go places."

"He isn't allowed to just up and abandon his responsibilities on a whim. I should have kept a closer eye on him," their father ranted arms waving.

"Father, he's not a child," Aethelric said with an incredulous expression on his face.

"Then he shouldn't act like one!" His father snapped, "clearly he can't be trusted to make the right choices."

Aelfraed stepped back from the stairs his hand on the rail. It creaked uncomfortably loud. Silence for a moment and then his father's head shot up, mirrored cold silvery blue eyes glaring at him. That judging gaze that he couldn't even escape in the mirror.

Reminding him how much he'd messed up, as if what he overheard hadn't.

"There you are! What were you thinking vanishing like that? I had half a mind to go to the Wardens," their father took a step onto the stairs.

Aelfraed stepped back, half tempted to run back up the stairs. He resisted that urge, his father would just follow. It would only make him angrier. There was no more running from his many mistakes.

Caoimhe pushed herself past onto the first step between them, "did I say you could go up there? Did Aethelric say you could come in for that matter?" There was a low warning tone to her voice, that set Aelfraed on edge.

His father glared his face managing to go redder. He opened his mouth.

"Sorry," Aelfraed said quickly cutting him off and drawing back his attention. He didn't want it but Caoimhe didn't deserve it.

"Sorry? Sorry doesn't cut it. You made me look like a fool. I had to drop everything to look for you. Throwing my efforts in the dirt when you should have been studying," He ranted, "and then you end up in the paper of all things. What were you thinking getting involved in something so dangerous?"

"You can't seriously expect him just to do nothing when something like that happens," Caoimhe said with a judging tone.

"He can barely manage the exams; chances are he made things worse not better. If he had stayed put it wouldn't have changed anything," he gestured at Aelfraed while glaring at Caoimhe for daring to question him.

"He's right there," she snapped.

"Its fine Caoimhe, he's right I probably messed something up," Aelfraed sighed, he took the remaining few steps down the stairs.

"Aelfie don't talk like that. You helped. Without you…" Aethelric placed a hand on his shoulder.

"No, no, I shouldn't have gotten involved," he shook his head, "I shouldn't have left in the first place. This whole thing was a mistake."

"You needed break Aelfie," Aethelric said.

"He needed to stay and study if he wants any chance at passing this time. We'll be heading back tomorrow," Their father said with a level of finality.

"He's not staying the night, Aelfraed can but I'm not putting up with him," Caoimhe crossed her arms and levelled their father with a glare.

Their father bristled, "of course I will be, how would it look if I was force to find somewhere to stay? I'd have to leave the dinner party early and then everyone would know."

"Wait, what dinner? I thought you were here because of Aelfraed," Aethelric questioned.

The question made Aelfraed thoughts pause, had his father already been planning on coming. Could he have had his break without the threat of getting caught this whole time? He would have still probably have needed to study but it would still have been something. Had he really gotten Aethelric into trouble for nothing?

"Would you rather it look like Aelfraed just ran off in the dead of night. Better the university think we've all just gone to visit an old friend," their father asked expecting them to want the same thing. He always did.

Aelfraed wasn't sure what he would rather, he didn't want to make his father look bad. He didn't want to let him down again. He was already very good at that. He didn't dare think about the part of him that only the other day had been so desperate for a break that he didn't care how it would look.

"We? Wait Caoimhe and I are not going anywhere," Aethelric snapped.

"You can't just storm into our house and demand we drop everything for you," Caoimhe said with an intense glare, her tone getting more and more angry. Aelfraed wondered if soon she would start shouting.

"Fine, you don't need to come. My sons are more than enough to assuage any rumours," the man said as if Aethelric had said nothing. Aelfraed hated when his father ignored Aethelric like that.

"Father, I said I wasn't going anywhere," he said again more firmly.

The man scowled at him, "you will do as I say. This isn't up for debate."

"Father, I am also not a child anymore. You can't just order me around,"

"Its fine, I'll go. You can just tell them Aethelric had work," Aelfraed spoke up, he hoped his ready agreement would take the pressure off Aethelric. He had to go anyway, it wasn't like he had a choice better to agree and hope that made things easier for everyone else at least.

Aethelric's head snapped round to look at Aelfraed, "oh no, Aelfie you are not going on your own."

Chapter Nine

Aelfraed tugged at the bottom of the borrowed shirt trying to tuck it into his trousers. As he pulled the runes that trimmed the hem, it shifted extending the shirt a little, the fabric thinning. There had been a time when he would have fitted Aethelric's clothes with ease but it had been years since then. As a result he was now wishing he had brought something a little smarter. Wearing what he had brought would only embarrass his father. His mood had been quelled somewhat with Aethelric and Caoimhe both agreeing to go but still the last thing he wanted was to let him down by dressing in a way that would make him look bad.

He looked down at himself, it would have to do. The shirt was a little old but not quite out of fashion. The cuffs were flared and the collar was short and didn't fold over.

He hoped that Aethelric had something left to wear himself. He felt bad enough that both he and Caoimhe had been forced to come. He'd tried insisting they didn't have to but neither had changed their mind. He hated that they had put things on hold so much just for him.

It was his fault that Aethelric had yet to get a chance to go visit Nira. He couldn't help but wonder what she would think. That Aelfraed just hadn't told him about what happened. Or that her friend was ignoring her.

Would she think that, he couldn't help but question. He wasn't sure. She didn't seem like the type to think badly of others. Still it was his fault even if she didn't think it was.

He shook his head breaking the spiral of thoughts. There was no time for that if he didn't want to make them all late. Finding the shirt had taken a good bit of time and there was nothing else that he could borrow beyond an old waistcoat that he was sure might have been their father's at one point. He didn't know how it had gotten into Aethelric's wardrobe.

There was nothing smarter in the way of trousers or shoes. Instead he wore the plain black brown trousers that he had brought with him. He'd wear the shoes he had travelled in, they weren't the worst. Practical and clean but not what would have been considered smart.

He glanced over to his comfortable blue and cream woollen cardigan, lying over the end of the bed. He wondered if he could get away with wearing it. It was cold out, he had felt the draft earlier and he didn't have a proper smart jacket just the long coat he had brought.

He slipped it on over the ruffled sleeves and had to fish up the sleeve to pull them down so that they would stick out from under the cuffs of the cardigan. It didn't look bad, a little casual but mixed well with the rest. It looked somewhat smart. Probably not enough for his father's liking. Maybe he shouldn't, he frowned starting to shrug it off of his shoulders. He didn't want to cause problems.

"Aelfraed!" He flinched at his father's bellow, "hurry it up! If you make me late…"

Aelfraed sighed, it would have to do. He didn't have time to find another jacket. He pulled it back over his shoulders and left the clasps so that his father could see that he was at least smartly dressed underneath it.

**

He headed down reluctant to confront the expected frown of his father at his choice of outfit. His family were waiting in the corridor below. Aethelric and Caoimhe were leaning against the wall near the door to the drawing room. Caoimhe wore a light blue shirt similar to the one the day before under the same navy blazer and with the same trousers. His brother was wearing a cream shirt with a dark brick red vest over the top with a high neckline that covered his shirt's collar with its own.

His father was tapping his foot impatiently. His slightly heeled black shoes tapped loudly off the wood. He was dressed in a traditional brown black blazer and high waisted trousers.

"Aelfraed..." the man started a new frown building on his face.

"Sorry father," Aelfraed interrupted flinching at the flashed glare, "there wasn't anything else."

"I'll be having none of that back talk once we're there," he snapped, "I suppose what you are wearing will have to do."

Aelfraed sagged as his father turned away towards the door. He had gotten off easy. He shouldn't have interrupted. After so many years he should have known better than that.

They headed out and at that point he was glad to have been able to keep the cardigan when they stepped into the cold air outside. The thick woven cardigan keeping him warm and cutting out the cold wind. He hooked the fastenings closed before jogging a few steps to catch up to his father's pace.

"How far are we going? Would it be easier if I called for a carriage?" Aethelric asked.

"No, no time for that thanks to Aelfraed's dawdling. We're taking the Step," the man grouched barely glancing back as he walked at a hastened pace.

Aelfraed frowned, was there really no time? Was a little late so bad? They could have just not gone. His father could have just said they were visiting Aethelric. Surely that would have been enough to save face with the university. While a family dinner would have been tense at least then they wouldn't have to face the scrutiny of their father's friends or even the Step. He wasn't sure which he was dreading more.

*

The Rune Step was a bustle of activity, a flow of people in and out the wide open doorways. Inside it was loud; conductors called out last calls for a Step. Familiar and unfamiliar locations being shouted across the large room. Aelfraed weaved through the crowd to keep up with the pace of his father, trying his best as he went to not bump into anyone.

Alcoves lined the walls, in them sat discs of red granite that stood out against smooth grey stone they were set into. Engraved with sharp lines resembling a compass with many extra points darting out all directions. Their edges worn down and the rune carvings rounded and chipped at the edges a little. People clustered on top of them. Some were standing while others sat on benches along the alcove wall.

Groups in the alcoves would vanish with a slight flare of light and the feeling of moving air that fluttered hair and clothes. The same in reverse for those that appeared in their place and then left the alcove into the mass of people heading for the doors. Aelfraed wished that was all it did. That there was nothing else to the Step.

Their father led them through the crowd to an alcove that led to the other side of the city. Few people standing already in it, less travelled than some of the other Steps.

The uniformed conductor called out for any remaining passengers. Aelfraed braced himself with a deep breath. A few moments later liquid poured into the channels made by the carvings. Running from the edges towards the middle then through narrow channels filling up the runes. As it crested the top of the channels the world lurched. His head spun. Aethelric caught his arm. The feeling of movement was gone as quickly as it had happened but in its wake it left him feeling rather unsteady. His stomach churning, head still spinning and ears ringing.

It felt no better than any previous time, no matter how many times people told him it would get easier. His family around him were no worse for wear. He knew Aethelric used to have it bad too but only a few times when they were younger. His father started moving immediately, shaking each shoe a little to clear off the few drops of liquid lingering from the Step. Aethelric supported him as they followed. They had told him before that it was just like blinking. They'd even suggested that he try to blink at the time of activation. Most didn't experience the disorientation, lack of balance or the sickness. At least not over such short distances, the longer ones could disorient even the best travellers.

The houses that lined the streets they walked through were a fair bit bigger than Aethelric's narrow townhouse. These houses stood separate with walled gardens around them big enough to fit more than a few planters.

As they approached the gate of one house there was a carriage standing nearby with an elderly man staggering out of it with the assistance of the driver. On the ground the man supported himself with a cane. A stained dark wood with a silver topper, the shape of which was hard to identify with the hand covering it. His hair was thin and greyed under a flat cap. His face was wrinkled in a way that made him look more cheery than grumpy. Silver trimmed spectacles covered his eyes with a shimmer. His suit was dark tweed and cut in an old style, his waistcoat more similar to the old one Aelfraed had found than Aethelric's or his father's current one. However still older style than that.

"Mr Odell! Good to see you," their father greeted the man who looked up, his eyes squinting with a moment of confusion.

"Ah, Mr Agmundrson. Good evening, who's this?" He questioned looking past their father to them.

"My sons, Aethelric and Aelfraed," their father said proudly as if he had not only hours ago been at odds with both of them.

The man squinted his eyes, behind his spectacles, "hmmm. I suppose I see the resemblance."

"You suppose? Maybe you need to get your spectacles looked at. They both take after me," their father said with a half joking laugh.

"I have been meaning to, you know how it is. Busy, busy," the man said jokingly.

They stepped through the gate into a nice well-kept garden with planted beds either side of the path. Mr Odell with his cane was a tad slower and instead of falling in step with their father he ended up keeping pace instead with Aelfraed, still unsteady from the Step.

"Take the Step?" The man asked as he squinted at Aelfraed.

"Yes, we were running a little late," Aethelric replied causing their father to flinch at the answer but he didn't contest it.

"Need a sweet? Won't do much but better than your stomach churning all night," Mr Odell asked as he dug his hand into the pocket of his jacket for the small bag.

Aelfraed smiled, "thank you."

"Not to worry, I know how the Step can be. Barely know how most of you young ones manage," he dropped a hard sweet into Aelfraed's hand.

"You get used to it Mr Odell," their father insisted, "Aelfraed just needs to use it more. Rather than wasting time with the alternatives."

"Those alternatives worked perfectly fine before, when people didn't bother with summons and the like for every little trip. Used to be a big deal to travel like that. Always something urgent," Mr Odell complained.

Aelfraed unwrapped the hard sweet and popped it in his mouth. It tasted of an uncertain sweet flavour. It did little as he sucked at it for the spinning in his head but he could feel the ease of the queasy rolling in his stomach. Even though he wasn't looking forward to the evening at least with this he would be able to stomach eating.

His father stepped up to the door that shimmered with its ward. Where Aelfraed would have knocked instinctively his father didn't move at all to do so.

Chapter Ten

The shimmer fizzled out and a smartly dressed man greeted them at the door with a nod and a momentary frown. His dark hair was brushed back and neat. He was in a simple yet smart dark grey suit that was ill-shapen and didn't fit the man quite properly. Either it was missing runes to adjust or they had long since worn out. There was a vague sense of familiarity about the man. It took Aelfraed a moment to realise this was the man he had seen shopping at the Bakery. The man showed not even a flicker of recognition however. The man led them through the hall after allowing a moment to slip off shoes in favour of house shoes.

"And then do you know what Gisel did?" Aelfraed could hear a conspiratorial voice as they gossiped.

"Aunty please..." someone else whined.

There was the sound of giggling, "you're embarrassing him Maggie."

Past a staircase and into a drawing room. The room was about twice the size of Aethelric's leaving plenty of space for movement between the furniture. A wide sofa sat opposite a coffee table with another smaller one to its left. Two armchairs finished the circle and beyond the table was a fireplace set into a polished stone cut chimney breast.

"Madam. Mr Odell, Mr Agmundrson and guests have arrived." There was an uncomfortable pause before guests. Aelfraed looked at the floor. Of course their father hadn't mentioned bringing them. He probably wouldn't have brought them at all if Aelfraed hadn't left the university. Would he have even come? It seemed like an afterthought to his father. Purely a way to save face and make himself look good than actually seeing a friend.

A woman sat in one of the armchairs. Her face crinkled a little with her smile as she stood. Her black hair was wound up in a mound of curls above her head that rather resembled a waterfall. The odd streak of silver only accentuated the effect. The streaks seemed more purposefully placed than the natural product of aging. She was dressed in long blue skirts that flowed down from a dark almost black bodice. All ending with white lace. Her puffed sleeves were the same blue and ended with a narrowed sleeve at her lower arm. The outfit looked well-worn and taken care of. The runes that trimmed it looked fresher than the fabric itself.

"Alexander!" She greeted enthusiastically, "take a seat, take a seat. Get yourself off that leg."

"Maggie, I'm fine. It's not as bad as you make out every time," he protested as he was lead to the sofa.

"That's because I make you sit down. Given half chance you'd stand all night," she scolded gently.

Once he had given in to being seated she turned back to them; that smile still on her face. Showing no signs of disapproval over the extra guests that their father had brought.

"Alvis, I wasn't expecting you to make it with your hands so full with academics on top of your clients. Giselbert will be so glad you made it," she said smiling at their father.

Their father puffed up with obvious pride. Aelfraed had seen it before, his father would be crowing about his many accomplishments all night. He hung back hoping that everyone would be too distracted to notice him as a result.

"Nothing I couldn't handle. When I made some time I thought I'd pop down considering Giselbert's invite. Hard to say no to your husband Magnolia. Thought I'd pay a visit to my eldest while I was in the city too," he said as if it was nothing.

"Oh so that makes these your boys? And this is? Your daughter? I didn't know you had one. You never mentioned her," she smiled as she looked over at them a note of confusion starting on her face.

He flinched and noticed as his father stiffened beside him. If it wasn't for the conversation between the two women on the other sofa they would have been left in an uncomfortable silence. His father's face began to redden. He braced himself and then before his father could react someone else did.

"Caoimhe, Caoimhe Agmundrson. It's nice to meet you. This is my husband Aethelric and his little brother Aelfraed," she said cutting off the uncomfortable gap.

The woman gave a light laugh having either not noticed the tension or chosen to ignore it, "of course, of course. I should have known. You really look nothing like him. I am Magnolia Drummond, a pleasure."

He breathed a sigh of relief as his father relaxed. The oppressive tension gone. Well not entirely, his father was still stony faced as she gestured to the sofas asking them to take a seat. Their father moved first joining the young man and Alexander. He had neat black hair and the same brown eyes as Magnolia. His face was squarer in the jaw and he had a round nose. Aethelric and Caoimhe joined the other sofa with the pair of women. Despite the four it wasn't too crowded with both couples sitting close to each other.

Aelfraed ended up perched awkwardly at the end of the sofa that his father had sat on.

Pushed into the corner and trying to take up as little space as possible. He did eye the gap on the other sofa between the couples but felt just as awkward at the idea of sitting himself between them.

"Emmett, could you let my husband know that his friend is here," Magnolia asked the man who had led them in.

Emmett had been almost out of the doorway and back into the hall. He froze and turned around, "yes, of course," he said quickly before heading off.

"I guess we're not hearing the rest of that story, ay Maggie?" One of the women said leaning forward; she gave the young man a light smirk along with a glance. He scowled and looked pleadingly at Magnolia.

Her dark brown hair was cut short above her shoulders, rather than the longer up styling that was common. She wore a strongly dyed goldenrod dress that faded into a more cream colour at the edges. Her arm was round the waist of the woman next to her. The other woman's brown hair was lighter and longer. Spectacles covered her hazel eyes that were pushed up with a soft happy smile. She wore a light long floral skirt topped with a cream puffed shirt.

"Sorry Elouise," she said with an amused smile, "maybe later?"

"Mr Agmundrson this is my nephew Iowerth and my friends Celia and Elouise," Magnolia introduced them.

"Mr Agmundrson used to be Giselbert's physician when we lived in Edinburgh," Magnolia explained.

"Oh you must meet a lot of people in that line of work. What do you do now?" Elouise asked curiously.

"Still a physician but more recently I have secured a post as the head of the Edinburgh University's healing department," their father said with a confident smile.

"He's no doubt rather proud of that," Aethelric commented. A dig at having not known before Aelfraed guessed from the tone.

"I would be too," Celia said the dig seeming going over her head, "what about you and Caoimhe?"

"Aethelric works for the courts and Aelfraed is currently studying in Edinburgh. He's going to be following in my footsteps," their father spoke before any of them could. He spoke proudly as if he hadn't only hours ago been berating Aelfraed for his failings.

Aelfraed frowned at the hypocrisy. He looked down at the floor as the conversation continued around him. Did his father even still want that or was it all for the show of it. He couldn't avoid Aethelric's question from the day he arrived, did he even want that.

"What about you Caoimhe," Elouise asked pointedly to a fed up looking Caoimhe.

"I work for the paper. Hoping to have my own column one day," she said with a determined look on her face.

"Oh I freelance for them occasionally. Took some photographs for tomorrow's edition only this morning," Elouise said.

"Really?" Caoimhe leant closer to Elouise, "what camera have you been using, I've been saving for one but all the technical and scientific stuff seems so complicated."

"Celia actually handles the chemistry side of it. I can work the machine but chemicals are not something I can understand," she explained, "maybe I can let you have some time with mine. Celia could develop the photographs."

"I can show you how the developing works but definitely complicated," Celia nodded.

The three continued to talk cameras and chemistry. Some of what they mentioned Aelfraed understood and others he didn't. He was curious but didn't want to speak up and draw attention to himself with a question. He didn't expect any of them would be against answering but his father would be irritated by the interest in something other than his studies. Beside him Magnolia and Alexander were catching up with his father. Talking of things that had happened since they had last seen each other. Aelfraed tuned it out.

"Oh what does Aethelric do for the courts?" Magnolia asked, Aelfraed wasn't sure when the conversation had changed course.

Aethelric looked up from where he had been just listening to Caoimhe's conversation. He laughed, "to be honest I'm not even sure of my job title anymore. I just end up involved with a bit of everything."

"Sounds like you're doing well over there then. In my day being the person that would get stuck in with anything was bound to get you further," Alexander said with some enthusiasm.

"You should take that attitude a bit more Iorwerth," Magnolia glanced over to her quiet nephew.

The man had been watching but saying nothing. Not since his complaints earlier. The way he twitched when she spoke made Aelfraed wonder if he wanted to be here as little as him.

"I do my studies, is that not enough?" He complained.

"Not if you want to get ahead. Some extra studies maybe?" Magnolia suggested, "wouldn't hurt to expand your horizons."

Iorwerth protested and Aethelric's attention turned to their conversation, "what are you studying?" He asked.

"Transmutation of..." Iorwerth began but was quickly cut off.

"Ah transmutation! A fascinating field. Though most of its applications are rather superficial," their father said.

Iorwerth frowned, his lips settling into a fed up expression, "it's not..."

"I would honestly recommend branching into the more healing related applications. Far more useful than the more cosmetic uses," their father continued.

Aelfraed directed his attention to the conversation about camera's happening on the other sofa to avoid being drawn into the very one-sided debate. He felt sorry for Iorwerth, he'd been on that side of his father's lectures before. Once he was talking about something he only heard the responses he wanted.

"Edinburgh has some excellent lecturers about that. I would recommend it, though being one of said lecturers I am quite biased."

Iorwerth tried one more time before giving up on actually participating in what had become Aelfraed's father telling Magnolia about the sorts of lectures offered by the university. Instead he discreetly reached for a book abandoned on the side table. Aelfraed eyed him jealously. He would have much rather been curled up at home with a book than here. Maybe at Aethelric's rather than home right now but still.

***

Before long another man arrived through the door to the room with a bright smile on his face and made a b-line for their father. He looked a little older than his father with more grey in his hair than in his wife's. It was combed neatly in a slight wave and a dark black brown. He was dressed smartly but not like he intended to join the party. A casual woven blazer over his cream shirt and dark coloured trousers. It made Aelfraed feel a little less out of place.

"Alvis! Ha, I knew you'd make it. After all with that terrible business the other day I supposed you'd visit before heading back to Edinburgh," he said clapping their father on the shoulder.

"Terrible business?" Questioned Elouise her attention drawn away from the discussion of cameras, before a dawning expression of understanding bloomed across her face, "oh wait. Agmundrson! I knew that sounded familiar. You were in the paper for assisting with that man that got attacked."

Their father's mouth split with a confident smirk. Revelling in the attention Aelfraed was glad wasn't on him. It was about him but maybe if he stayed quiet, let them think it was his father then he wouldn't have to recant the events of that day. His father would probably take the credit after all. Rather than letting any of it fall to him. He frowned, why did that make him mad? He didn't want the attention.

"Actually that was Aelfraed. If he hadn't been there who knows it would have been worse," Caoimhe piped up dragging the attention of Aelfraed's father and right on to him.

He felt his face warm and he kept his eyes on the polished wood floor. This wasn't what he had wanted. He most definitely had not wanted the attention on him. Even though he couldn't see them he was sure eyes were on him.

"No no, Caoimhe please. It wasn't that big of a thing. It was more Physician Caldwell," he said shaking his head.

"You must be proud of such a responsible young man," Giselbert congratulated their father.

"Yes, yes I'm very proud. A chip off the old block. I would have done no differently," he crowed proudly.

The words only added to the building frustration. He hated how two faced the man could be. Berating one minute and the next singing praises. It had long ago started churning an uncertainty in Aelfraed. An uncertainty of if he was ever good enough. Ever doing the right thing.

He glanced up and caught sight of Aethelric's accusing glare at their father. Aelfraed shook his head lightly hoping his brother would see. He didn't want to cause a scene. Not here, not now. He didn't want Aethelric to get himself into trouble over something he should be able to deal with himself, whatever way of dealing with it that became.

"Maybe we should send Iorwerth back with you. Such an upstanding young man would be a good influence. Maybe even extend those transmutation studies," Giselbert didn't even look at Iorwerth as he spoke to their father.

"I was just saying the same thing," Magnolia said happily.

"Uncle," Iorwerth started to protest.

"I'm sure that's a decision for Iorwerth to make," Aethelric said accusingly from across the room, "right father?"

There was an uncomfortable silence as their father started to go red in the face. He could see the man's mouth turn into a scowl as he tried to stop himself from reacting. Aelfraed tried to keep out of line of sight, despite what had been said he knew this was about him. He didn't know how Aethelric managed to say things like that so boldly.

Chapter Eleven

Magnolia shifted in her seat to glance at the grandfather clock against the wall. The hands pointed to half past seven. A frown crossed her face. She was about to stand when there was an attention seeking hum from the doorway, that cut off the awkward lull in the conversation. Aelfraed breathed a sigh of relief.

"Dinner is served," Emmett said stood in the doorway. He shifted awkwardly under the now judging gaze of Magnolia.

After a moment as they got up from their seats conversation returned. Some only saying the odd word or two while Elouise and

Caoimhe were back into a discussion on styles of photography. Aelfraed kept his head down and lingered toward the back. He hoped the distraction of food would keep them from asking more questions about what happened.

Emmett led them through from the drawing room and into a dining room that was far bigger than Aethelric's one that only sat four before becoming cramped.

Aelfraed only sat down himself after his father had also found his seat. He ended up between his father and the now even quieter Iorwerth who seemed to be avoiding his uncle as much as Aelfraed wanted to be able to avoid his father. He had hoped to have some sort of buffer between him and his father. Not Caoimhe or Aethelric. He was glad that they had been pulled by the conversation to the other side of the table. Alexander would have been enough. Someone who actually seemed to like the man.

Aelfraed tuned out the soft chatter around the table as the dinner was served. He hadn't wanted to be there before and now he wanted it even less. He didn't even feel all that hungry. That was probably nerves or the lingering feeling of the Step. He picked slowly at the served food more for politeness's sake than anything else. He wondered if everyone else was just being polite. It wasn't bad. The light coloured soup tasted just as much of squash as expected for the colour but it was plain. At the university he'd been mostly living off of food from the cafeteria. Quick simple and could be eaten at speed. This struck him as like that. Also familiar rather than a more tailored recipe. There was also an absence of rolls but if Emmett had been ordering them at the Bakery that day it made sense that he didn't get them.

Emmett came and went through out the dinner. Out and then back to refill drinks. Then gone again until the main course.

*_**

By the time they were onto dessert Aelfraed had resorted to just moving the food round the plate. He had gone past not hungry and was now at the point of not being able to eat another bite.

Beneath the chatter there was a whine, like a ringing in his ears and he wondered if he was imagining it. His eyes glanced up to the ring of light runes carved into the wood of the ceiling, glowing a soft flame yellow. He sometimes wondered if it was the flow of magic he was hearing when his mind wandered and picked up on that sort of sound. He frowned as it seemed to grow louder, more intense or maybe it was just because he was thinking about it. Someone tapped his arm, trying to get his attention.

The light grew sharp, suddenly brighter. A faint smell of burning wood. Then they were plunged into darkness with the sound of splintering wood. A cascade of clattering and the odd smash as fragments of ceiling hit the table. A series of yelps and scraping chairs; then a light relieved laughter.

Aelfraed couldn't even see his hand in front of his face. The lamps of the street beyond the garden walls not bright enough to cast light in through the windows.

"Some light please Emmett," Magnolia's voice called out of the dark.

There was a few footsteps and a cry of pain as the table shook. A loud thump as something, probably a chair hit the floor. Maybe two. Yet no light appeared.

"Will someone make some light already?" He heard his father snap.

Aelfraed frowned and raised a hand. He hummed out a few words focusing on the light blooming from it. It wasn't bright enough to reach the corners of the room but still cast light across the table revealing their host and the other guests. Their faces cast in hollowing shadows. The table was a mess of scattered bits of broken wood and the remains of the meal.

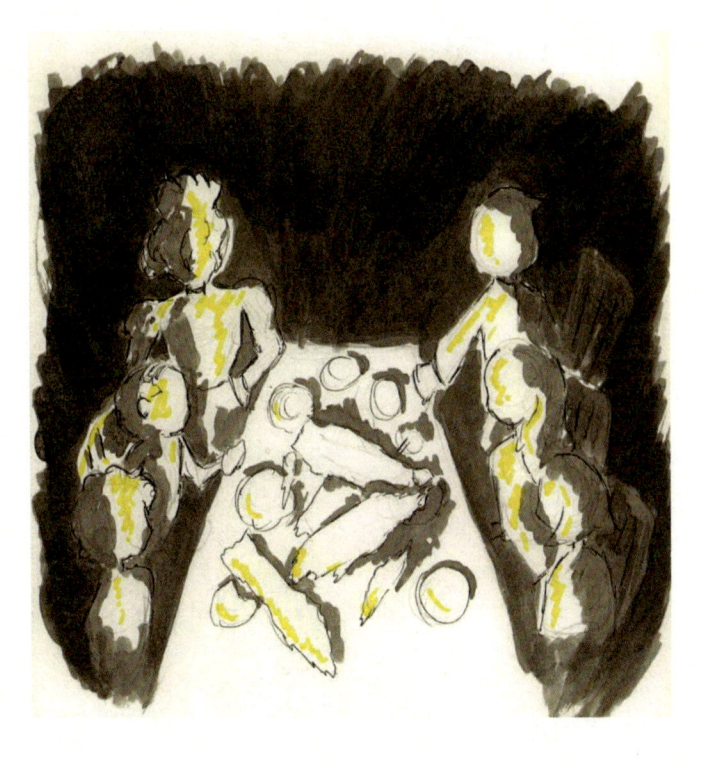

Even in the half-light the shadows were not big enough to hide the two missing men. Emmett who had been by the door moments earlier and Giselbert who's empty chair lay on the floor, just visible past the table.

Magnolia looked round, "where is that man? What am I paying him for?" she said with frustrated sigh.

She froze, her shadow cast face paled and contorted. She dropped to the floor screaming.

"Whats going on? What happened?" Their father questioned as he charged over, dragging Aelfraed over with the light.

Blood. The light flickered out, the simple concentration lost. It was more than just a little blood. He hadn't just grazed a knee from the impact with the table. Aelfraed couldn't see it with the renewed dark but he couldn't forget what he had seen. Giselbert lying on the floor, blood welling up from a large wound in his chest. A hand clutched at it. Blood spluttering with each breath. Breaths that he could still hear. Wheezing like the Baker. The smell of smoke was in his nose. Breathing like she hadn't been.

His father jerked his arm sharply and shook him, "Pull yourself together. Get that light back up."

Aelfraed took a deep breath trying to calm himself. His voice shook as he tried to keep a light going. Repeating the chant despite the simplicity of the spell. The light flickered. Caoimhe's voice spoke up from the other side of the table with a similar spell. A small orb of light floating above them directed by her pointing finger. She didn't move closer. She had a steeled expression on her face and was keeping her eyes trained on the ceiling and not the blood pooling on the wood floor that slowly crept out from where it was hidden by the table.

Aelfraed's father pulled him harshly down to the ground before finally releasing his grip. Instead moving to place his hands either side of the stab wound. He started without hesitation on a spell.

Aelfraed stared at the wound his mind reeling. It was deep and welled with blood. Deeper than anything he had dealt with before in practice. Jagged as if someone had pulled the knife away as he fell. All he could see was her. Her body covered in blood. He harshly shook away the thought that he had had too many times for such a short few days. He tried to steady his breath, he couldn't spiral. Not here. Not now. Again the body before him was still breathing.

She haunted him as he placed his hands either side of his father's. Rightful self-doubt creeping in. This was beyond him. Beyond his skills. Again he was out of his depth.

Blood soaked his cuffs as it welled over his hands. His words trailed a little behind his father as he mimicked the more advanced spell to the best of his abilities. It was a spell much closer to the transmutation roots of the more modern healing spells. Not just telling the body to heal as it would naturally just faster but forcing it back where it would have never naturally healed. It required a knowledge of anatomy that was beyond those without some expertise. Many would have been able to heal a simple small cut or scrape. However for such a large wound without that understanding there was a strong chance that something would go back wrong only hastening the man's demise.

Aelfraed fought to focus on what he had learnt. How more complex injuries would heal but he lacked the practical experience. Even as he felt the strain of the magic he knew that his father was very much carrying the greater effort.

"Take over," his father barked.

Aelfraed stuttered over the loop for a moment before falling into his own rhythm. No time to pause to protest. He was thankful that he had at least heard the full chant once through. It was easier to repeat at that point. However it had lost a lot of its power with the loss of his father's expert knowledge. The shifting healing under his hands slowed.

"We need more light," he bellowed over the table at caoimhe on the other side.

"Right," she replied quickly. A muttered word and the light grew brighter.

His father chanted through another loop of the spell, far faster than Aelfraed's own. He didn't dare shift to keep pace and potentially loose his own focus.

"Wardens, get the wardens," their father barked out another order on finishing the loop.

"Already on their way!" Aethelric called out.

"Another physician too! Someone actually trained!" Their father added. Aelfraed tried to ignore the jab at his skills. He couldn't afford the distraction. It wasn't exactly unwarranted.

"Also done," he heard Aethelric snap.

His father fell into another loop of the spell, his eyes on the healing wound. The flesh crept slowly together. Not fast enough for the slowing beat beneath their hands.

"Not good enough. You three! I need a rune circle," he shouted for Celia, Elouise and Iorwerth.

Aelfraed shook his head and stared hard at the wound. Trying to think of nothing else but anatomy and the looping chant of the spell as his father walked the others through drawing out the correct runes. Loud instruction became just loud. Still jarring but not at the front of his attention.

∗

Soon his father's hands joined his again. Starting up with another spell. More complicated and with a faster pace. Aelfraed tried his best to match it. The strain multiplying too, a headache building. He could feel the energy running through his hands. He tried not to think about the building warmth. He pushed past a slow blink and forced himself to stare at the shifting skin around his hands. He didn't want to look but after days of not enough food or sleep and an awful lot of stress he couldn't afford to be distracted. He couldn't let exhaustion set in yet.

The energy draining sensation of the spell stuttered and failed. The man's chest stilled beneath their hands. That wasn't meant to happen. It had been working and then, nothing. Had he messed up? Had he stumbled over his words the wrong way? Had he somehow made it worse? He could hear yelling, wailing. His father booming at him.

He'd done it again. He'd messed up again. All these years and he was still useless. What good was he? He stared at his bloody hands as he was pulled away by a firm grip at his shoulders.

⁎

He heard the rumble of thunder or was that drums. It did his pounding head no favours. Thunder and rain would be an appropriate thing. Rain to wash off all the blood. Maybe footsteps off wood? He thought he could hear more voices than before.

Magnolia's wailing had softened into rough sobs and he could hear the distant voices around him. A hand touched his. A pair of voices one familiar and another only vaguely. His father was making demands he couldn't hear properly somewhere. Expected. When was his father not demanding something of someone? Demanding they come to the party. Demanding Aelfraed come back with him.

He didn't want to.

"Mr Agmundrson…" someone was talking to his father.

"Aelfraed? Aelfie? You're okay. We're okay. The Wardens are here," Aethelric's voice cut through his muddled thoughts.

"Aelfraed?" Came another voice, the one less familiar.

Something was wafted in front of his face, it smelt strongly of herbs. He recognised it from the morning after late night study sessions. Not coffee but a mix meant to help with awareness.

His heavy breathing brought a harsh lung full of the smell in. It caught on his throat revealing a rawness left over from the rough air of the Bakery. He coughed harshly leaning forward. He blinked; he wasn't sure when he had made it across the room. Aethelric stood with a hand on his shoulder as he caught his breath and next to him was the familiar face of the Warden from the other day, Wynnstan.

The room behind them was now lit with a scattered array of hastily drawn runes across the walls. The chairs had been pushed back around the body allowing the Wardens access. He tried his best not to look at the body. Instead focusing on the faces of the unknown Wardens that were scattered about the room. Most clustered at the end of the table and the body that had him instantly averting his eyes to another part of the room.

Magnolia was sat in one of the pushed back chairs, pale with bright red tear tracks down her cheeks. Alexander stood facing her as almost a barrier to her seeing the body still on the floor. Behind her was Elouise and Celia, Elouise had one hand on Magnolia's shoulder in a comforting grip and the other held Celia's. Aelfraed couldn't hear the words but the three were exchanging softly spoken whispers.

Iorwerth stood off on his own in a shocked sort of silence looking blankly at the wall.

Aelfraed wondered how long he had been stood there like that. Caoimhe eyed him from where she stood talking to one of the Wardens.

Warden O'Darachir stood glaring up at the taller man that was their father. Aelfraed didn't know what had started it but it was clear one of them had set the other off.

"O'Darachir? I'm going to take the Agmundrson's outside a moment. I think Aelfraed needs some air,"Wynnstan called over.

Caiomhe paused her conversation and leaned to one side to add, "maybe take Iorwerth with you if you can. I think he needs it too,"

"Air?" his father scoffed, "that boy needs to get his act together. It's not like this will be the last time he looses a patient."

Aelfraed couldn't help but notice Iorwerth flinching along with him. Was it just the shout, what was said or did Iorwerth blame him too.

"Patient!" Magnolia shrieked, "how dare you talk about Giselbert like that! Like he was just another client. You were meant to be his friend Alvis!"

"Now Magnolia, I'm just trying to stay calm about all this. A murder scene is not the place to mourn," his father held up his hands placating.

"Fine, take them outside," O'Darachir said loud enough to cut them both off without actually shouting. His brows furrowed with irritation, "take the three of them. I'll deal with this," he finished nodding to Aelfraed's father and Magnolia who looked one wrong word away from descending back into the argument.

Aelfraed didn't blame her. Aelfraed's fault or not it was cold to talk about his friend that way.

***

Wynnstan stood up and offered Aelfraed a hand. The four staggered outside into the cold air. An uncomfortable mirror of only the other day. Aelfraed shivered in the dark. They sat on the step.

"So what happened? O'Darachir's going to get it from inside but I might as well get your side out here. Quieter that way," Wynnstan asked as he drew light runes onto the ground in a couple of places, helping to alleviate the dark.

"It was meant to be Aunt Maggie's birthday party... some party..." Iorwerth tried to start, he seemed unsure what to even say.

"We're sorry about your Uncle, we'll figure out what happened. Does that mean everyone here was a friend of Magnolia's?" Wynnstan asked.

Iorweth shook his head, "their father," he gestured to Aelfraed and Aethelric, "he was really uncle's friend. Aunt Magnolia liked him but I wouldn't say they were friends. After what happened in there I don't think they are if they were."

Wynnstan nodded, "okay, so then what happened during dinner?"

"We were having dessert when the light runes blew through the ceiling. Giselbert was fine before then. It must have happened before Aelfraed created a light. Something knocked the table and I think we heard Giselbert fall. After that is was all hands on deck trying to save him," Aethelric explained his voice was shaken too.

"Alright, thank you. Did you notice anything else?" He asked starting to take notes.

There was something else. He wondered if Aethelric had even noticed in the chaos, "Emmett, the butler, I think. Magnolia called for him to make a light but he wasn't there. He was gone," Aelfraed added, he was worried. There was a murderer somewhere and either the missing person was also dead or they did it.

Aethelric's face dropped more into concern, "right, I forgot. He didn't even appear after Magnolia started screaming," Aethelric said, "Surely he would have come running if he had heard, do you think he's alright."

Iorwerth's eyes narrowed, "He'd only been hired this week, you don't think…"

"We don't know anything yet. He might not have done anything. Though we best get back inside and make sure O'Darachir knows," Wynnstan said standing up.

"Aelfie, Iorwerth you ready to go back in," Aethelric asked, he looked at them both concerned.

"I'd let you stay out here but O'Darachir's going to have questions so best if you are. If not I can send someone else out to sit with you," Wynnstan offered, it was an appealing one.

He imagined that they would all really rather stay out here. The cold was only a little unpleasant. However that would also put more strain on the Warden's investigations. They'd have to send someone out every time there was another question.

"No no, no need. I'll come with you. I'll be fine," Aelfraed decided. He didn't want to make things harder on the Wardens.

"The same, I can cope. For now at least," Iorwerth said.

"Are you sure, that was your Uncle. I understand if you need more time," Wynnstan asked with a tone of uncertainty.

"I know, I'm sure, I can manage," Iorwerth insisted.

Chapter Twelve

"O'Darachir, we have a missing person," Wynnstan said the moment they returned to the dining room.

O'Darachir turned his head quickly, a hand going up to cut off Alexander who he had been speaking with, "who?" he asked.

"Emmett, a staff member," Wynnstan answered.

"You didn't mention him," O'Darachir said looking back to the others.

"I… I'd forgotten. He was only hired this week so I could plan the party. I… we couldn't afford someone full time. With what happened I'd completely forgotten," Magnolia explained through her shaky voice, still sounding on the edge of crying.

"I thought Giselbert's work had been going well?" Aelfraed's father asked.

"Not as well as we all would have liked," she responded snippily, "it had to have been him. No one else would. Everyone loved my husband."

Iorwerth nodded, "it must have been."

"He must have slipped out while we were still in the dark," Alexander agreed.

"Well what are you Wardens waiting for? Find the murderer," his father insisted, raising his voice impatiently.

O'Darachir scowled, "fan out. Search the house and the gardens. I'll contact the keep to send Wardens to search the nearby streets. As long as he didn't make it to the Step we should be able to find him fairly easily."

The Wardens filed out leaving only O'Darachir and Wynnstan with them. O'Darachir turned with that frustrated scowl back on his face. The same as the one from his arrival at the Bakery.

"What do you know about this Emmett?" He asked, the glare directed at Magnolia.

His glare was met by others from Magnolia's friends who pushed closer together. It was a little callus to put her on the spot after what happened.

"I... not much. I put out a notice in the paper. He seemed respectable enough... I knew I should have doubted it," Magnolia explained as she continued to cry.

"Why?" Wynnstan asked.

She looked at the floor, "this... this is my fault."

"No. No Maggie it isn't," Celia grabbed her hands, crouching in front of her.

"No it is. I should have known. I should have been suspicious," she pulled her hands away, "he... he didn't have any recommendations."

"Maggie, why hire him then? That isn't like you," Elouise asked her voice raised with confusion.

"He... he spun what was probably a made up sob story of needing the money. I... I wanted to help and it... it was just for the party. I just wanted to help... and spend time with... Giselbert," she sobbed harshly through every word.

*

The sound of scuffling and protesting voices cut off the continued questioning some time later. It was moments from the start of the sounds to the appearance of a pair of Wardens dragging Emmett through the door. His hair was no longer neat and his jacket had been discarded at some point.

"We found him passing silverware over the fence. His associates got away. Ran the moment we spotted them," one of the Wardens explained.

"Silverware?" Wynnstan asked looking confused.

"Yes, the kitchen is stripped. Wouldn't be surprised if other rooms have been," the Warden confirmed with a nod.

"Wait, why are you confused? Of course I took the silverware I'm a thief. What did you expect? You caught me? Isn't that why you're here? Maggie came looking and noticed stuff missing right? Right?" He asked confusion turning into something more on his face as he looked from the Wardens, to Magnolia and then finally to the covered body on the floor. He froze up, staring, "what happened?"

"Mr Drummond was murdered." O'Darachir answered bluntly.

"He… was what?" Emmett stuttered, "wait, you don't think I did it? I didn't, it wasn't me."

"Just admit it, you did it. Giselbert probably walked in on you stealing. You were just trying to cover your tracks," their father accused.

"Mr Agmundrson would you please let us do our job, rather than jumping to conclusions," O'Darachir had clear frustration in his voice.

"Then do it. Arrest him!" He insisted.

"I will but first I have some questions. Did Mr Drummond catch you?" O'Darachir asked looking back to Emmett.

"Of course not! You'd have already been called if I had been seen. No way he would have let me just keep at it," Emmett exclaimed.

"Giselbert was with us the whole time after Emmett went to get him. He didn't seem angry in anyway or like something had happened," Aelfraed said remembering how pleased the man had been to see his father. How cheery he had been, he wondered just how well the two had really known each other considering the mask his father often put on to show a good side to the world. On top of how the man was acting now in the wake of Giselbert's death.

"He was clearly trying to find an opportunity without ruining Magnolia's event. Leave this to those who actually know what they are doing Aelfraed," his father scolded.

Aelfraed looked away trying not to be caught in a glare or the roll of his eyes. Hypocrite. Only moments ago his father was sticking his own oar in.

"Like Uncle would have let that stop him," Iorwerth said bitterly, "he'd have summoned the Wardens without hesitation if he knew. He wasn't the type to let something like this even slide for a moment."

"Maybe you should take your own advice," O'Darachir commented with a look at Aelfraed's father.

"What was the evening like for you?" Wynnstan asked Emmett.

"I turned up, pretended to prep food. I'd spent the weekend spending the budget on something pre-prepared. I'm no cook," Emmett explained with a little desperation.

"Why not just make off with the budget? If you wanted money wouldn't that be easier?" Wynnstan asked.

"Boss figured we'd get more out of the house with Magnolia distracted," he explained, "wish I had honestly right now."

"Don't call her that. You don't deserve to!" Alexander growled moving between them with a groan at his leg protesting.

Magnolia eyed his leg, "Alexander, you... you shouldn't push yourself," she muttered, worried but without the strength that she insisted with before.

"Fine. Whatever Mrs Drummond then," he raised his hands the best he could with his arms held by the Wardens, "look I feel bad about this but business is business. No one was meant to get hurt. Everyone was fine. I served dessert and then headed outside. Get the last of the stuff and bail. Or at least that was the plan."

"You can't really believe that. Clearly he did it," his father ranted.

"I will believe what there is evidence of," O'Darachir said with a pointed look.

"This was probably meant to be just another distraction," Alexander said.

"Considering your associates did just that we can't be sure you had nothing to do with it. Sit him down and make sure he doesn't go anywhere," O'Darachir instructed.

The Wardens dragged him over to one of the stood up chairs and forced him to sit. Celia moved cautiously over to Elouise's other side.

They used their cuffs to fasten his wrists to the back of the chair. The flat metal band deforming to wrap round his wrists and the bars of the chair.

"Check him for any weapons," O'Darachir ordered, "the victim was sitting just in front of the door. He could have easily stabbed him and then fled. Using the darkness to cover his tracks."

"He was probably trying to grab the good silver right off the table," Iorwerth said, "look, Uncle's knife is missing."

He pointed to the place setting nearest the door. The forks and spoons remained but the knife was absent. Aelfraed glanced under the table, nothing. Nothing but the blanketed body he didn't want to look at. It seemed to be the only thing missing off the table. The candle stands were still at the centrepiece with the silver tray. The remaining silverware at each seat. He paused to look at an indistinct cone like metal shape that looked like it might have been an unused candle holder broken by the falling ceiling or a broken ornament. Poorly made with a wobbly uneven shape that made him wonder if it had sentimental value.

"There is a Knife," one of the Wardens called as they pulled a sharp definitely not silverware knife from in Emmet's belt.

"Well that is that," the other said, "Mr Drummond must have caught him reaching for the cutlery in the dark."

"What oh come on, of course I have a knife. Be stupid not to but that doesn't mean I did it," Emmett struggled in his seat.

It made sense. Or at least it would have if it wasn't for the fact that he couldn't have blown the light runes without touching them. Any of them would have seen him if he had tried. He remembered smelling the smoke. It seemed to perfect to have been an accident. He didn't even think Emmet had been in the room when he had smelt the burning.

"Warden... sorry but Emmett didn't touch the runes. To blow them like that he'd have to. I don't think he was even in the room," Aelfraed spoke up looking at O'Darachir. His confidence boosted by knowing the man had listened to him at the Bakery.

"Aelfraed..." his father warned.

"Let him talk, that is the whole point Mr Agmundrson," O'Darachir cut him off, "hard to run an investigation if the witnesses don't tell us what they know."

Aelfraed eyed his father warily, there was a deep scowl and he was glaring while turning slowly red. He wondered how much longer his father could go with completely losing his temper. Aelfraed wasn't looking forward to the man reaching breaking point.

O'Darachir looked up at the hole in the ceiling and then round the room, "is there one on the wall, would be a bit awkward to stand on the table every time," O'Darachir asked, looking for it himself.

"Yes it's just over there. He's right we'd have seen him near it," Magnolia pointed out the unlit rune that was carved into the wall a little away from the doorway.

"He would have had to have stood there for a while too. I could smell burning before the lights even got much brighter," Aelfraed explained.

"An unrelated accident then?" Wynnstan asked.

"Can't have been... or at least I think it's unlikely. The chances of it lining up like that, you know," Aelfraed was less certain as he spoke, he didn't want to jump to conclusions like his father had been doing.

"When were the runes last drawn?" Wynnstan asked Magnolia.

"Only last week," she answered quickly.

"The rune tech was probably part of his gang that ran off," Iorwerth said.

"You think we'd be stealing if we could do anything like that. I'd take a normal job over this crap," Emmett exclaimed.

"Why didn't you, you could have just done the job and gotten paid. Probably a recommendation too even if you still faked the cooking," O'Darachir asked.

"Wouldn't have lasted. Sooner or later I'd be back to the gang," Emmett sighed, "only so long you can fake it you know."

Aelfraed's eyes were drawn back to the table as he pointedly tried to not look at the body. Looking around was a fair distraction as long as he didn't look at the covered shape.

There was something odd about the fragments of wood on the table. He'd sort of noticed it before but assumed that it was just the runes that allowed the magic to flow from the rune on the wall up to the array of them on the ceiling. However now he looked again the runes on the rough side of the wood were far more complicated than would be needed to connect them to the rune on the wall.

Aelfraed stepped forward picking up a larger wooden fragment off of the table. He turned it over to look at the twisting black sooty marks of burn through runes. With such small fragments he couldn't identify the use of the marks.

"Hey you shouldn't really be touching that. I mean I know you did with the shirts at the Bakery but still," Wynnstan said quickly when he spotted him.

"Sorry," he said putting it down quickly. He looked guiltily at the floor. He hadn't meant to cause trouble. He'd been so distracted he hadn't even thought about it. However he had seen something he should at least mention, proof that the runes had been tampered with, "I just noticed the runes, they're more than should be there. These runes must have been sending more power to the light rune than normal. Burning through the wood and causing it to break."

"Its fine, just more paper work," O'Darachir brushed it off, "a bit like the protection runes at the Bakery then. What's above us?"

The lack of irritation on O'Darachir's face was a relief. His expression was more once of focus than the frown and deepening lines on the brow that he had been worried about seeing. The man walked over to the table beside him and looked over the fragments. Aelfraed felt less guilty knowing that he hadn't really caused much of a problem.

"Just a spare room," Magnolia answered softly, "It... used to be my sister's."

"Your sister?" Wynnstan asked.

Celia's hand tightened on Magnolia's shoulder in a comforting gesture and Aelfraed noticed Alexander glance towards Iorwerth. Iorwerth stood a little away and avoided the eye contact. His eyes falling to the floor as he noticed the glance.

"Yes... my sister, his mother," she gestured towards Iorwerth, "they moved in with us when money was tight a few years back. She... she got sick."

Aelfraed winced, that explained why she hadn't been present. He couldn't help but feel sorry for Magnolia, to have to relive that while also dealing with another tragedy. Maybe she had noticed the tension when she had mistaken Caoimhe for his sister.

"Oh I see, I'm sorry," Wynnstan quickly apologised.

"Does that mean you live here?" O'Darachir asked looking over to Iorwerth.

Iorwerth nodded but didn't speak. O'Darachir looked back up to the hole in the ceiling after making a note in his book, "We'll need to see that room," O'Darachir said, "Are any of you in a fit state to show us which one?"
He looked over the people more familiar with the house, his eyes lingering more on Magnolia and Iorwerth. While Magnolia was still very much visibly shaken Iorwerth was in a more silent distant shock.

"I can show you up there," Iorwerth spoke up, finally looking towards them rather than the corner, "I'd take any chance to be away from here," Iorwerth's eyes lingered on the covered body that Aelfraed was avoiding.

"Wynnstan stay here to watch the room, Mr Agmundrson do you think you can tell us more about that rune if you saw the lot of it? Would save calling for an expert," O'Darachir asked.

"Of course I can," Aelfraed's father said quickly, for the first time in a while looking less red and shoulders pushed higher.

"Ah I was asking for the younger," O'Darachir corrected, his father stuttered and looked confused.

"Me?" Aelfraed questioned wondering for a moment if he was talking about Aethelric but then realised that O'Darachir didn't really know him, "why? I mean I know I was of some help last time but..."

"Last time!" His father shouted before remembering he had an audience, "Wardens, Wardens please don't be foolish. Whatever help he was last time was a fluke. He's not going to be any use."

Aelfraed flinched away from his father. It didn't hurt to hear that dismissal again as much as he thought it would.

"You've sure changed your tune," Alexander said leaning on his cane with both arms, "you are clearly not who I thought you were Mr Agmundrson."

"I believe I was asking your son not you. Aelfraed? Correct? Best I know to save your father the embarrassment of a repeated mistake," O'Darachir said with more rather direct bite than previously.

"Excuse me!" His father's face was scarlet, he seemed torn. Not knowing if he wanted to defend himself more against O'Darachir or Alexander's words.

Aelfraed eyed his father warily, with how red he looked he wondered if the man would faint before he exploded. He'd never raised a hand but words could be just as bad. He glanced quickly to O'Darachir who was waiting for an answer. He wasn't sure what that answer was. He might but also he might not. He nodded deciding that whatever the case he wanted out of this room. Away from his father.

"Yes, I'm not sure how much help I'll be but I'll try," he said.

"That's fine. We can always call an expert in after if you're not certain," Wynnstan reassured.

He couldn't help but send his brother and Caoimhe an apologetic glance as they started to move. He didn't want to leave them with their father in this state. Iorwerth led them from the dining room, carefully skirting around the body that still lay on the floor. Aelfraed imagined it would have been removed if so many of the Wardens hadn't been sent off after the thieves. His father had looked livid, and as they left he could hear the start of a loud argument as he turned on what had been at least supposedly his friends.

**

Iorwerth led them out back into the hallway, and nodded down the hall in the direction of the stairs that headed up into the rest of the house. The floor above dark. Aelfraed wondered if the runes had managed to burn out all of the house's runes or if they had just been extinguished before Giselbert came down. Iorwerth called a light as they started onto the first step of the stairs.

"I'm sorry about my father, it would be better if you didn't rile him up like that. I'm sure he could have helped more than me," Aelfraed said to O'Darachir. He was sure O'Darachir could hold his own in a shouting match with his father at this point but he would rather it not get to that.

"You don't need to apologise for him. I have my reasons for asking you over him," O'Darachir said.

"Why?" Aelfraed couldn't help but ask, had he really given the impression at the Bakery that he knew a lot about this sort of thing. If he had then O'Darachir was going to be at least a little disappointed.

"He annoys me, you don't," O'Darachir said plainly, "and you are more likely to tell it to me straight if you don't know."

It was true, his father wasn't good at the truth if it made him look bad but it didn't mean he wasn't more knowledgeable. He was more experienced and studied. Maybe more specialised over Aelfraed's own random curiosity driven knowledge but surely he had picked up things over the years. It was probably that curiosity of his that caused him to be unable to keep up after all. Just too distracted by irrelevant things. It was the reason he had messed up. The reason he had failed.

"He's still more likely to know... I wouldn't want to steer you wrong," Aelfraed said, "I already messed up..."

"Stop. Stop right there," O'Darachir did that very thing half way onto the next step. He levelled Aelfraed with a firm look. "I'm not dealing with a pity party. I need the Aelfraed from the Bakery. You know the one that keeps rearing his head every time you start thinking. A little nervous is fine but completely tearing yourself down over this isn't going to help."

Aelfraed didn't know how to respond. He stared, his mouth opening and closing. One part of him wanted to continue to protest. An automatic part so used to not being useful. Another wanted to agree, at least about tearing himself up over it. He wanted to help. He wanted to at least try.

"Right..." Aelfraed nodded.

"Good now let's go. Maybe show him what you're really capable of hmm," O'Darachir said as he started walking again.

"It's through here," Iorwerth said as he led them down a corridor and stopping at a door.

***

Inside the room smelt strongly of burnt wood. A small beam of light came from the hole. As they approached it they heard yelps from below and the scattered sound of debris falling. The floor boards creaked, shifting.

"Everyone alright?" Aelfraed called down worried that someone might have gotten hurt.

"Yes, just ashes and splinters," Wynnstan's voice came up through the floor, "mostly on the table anyway."

Aelfraed and O'Darachir's called lights joined Iorwerth's as they glanced round the room. The light pushed away the dark further allowing them to see more. The floor was a bare wood and the furniture had been pushed to the edges. Not like it was being used as storage but as if the things had been moved recently, the bed still made and hand prints in the dust that had settled in the time it wasn't used. The only thing clear of dust was an area of the floor around the hole.

"It wasn't like this before," Iorwerth said as he waved his light round the room as he turned, "it's normally at least set up for guests."

"When were you last in here?" O'Darachir asked.

"Not for months," he said, "I have a room further down the hall."

"Seen anyone else come in?" O'Darachir asked.

"No," he shook his head, "we've not had guests for a while so Aunt Maggie wouldn't have braved it for cleaning."

"Magnolia? Have you been in this room recently?" O'Darachir called.

The response was quiet and Aelfraed was certain that O'Darachir had missed it too by the look on his face.

"Could you repeat that?"

"She said no O'Darachir," Wynnstan called up.

O'Darachir frowned, "someone must have been. We'll take a look at the rune and then head back down. Save the need for Wynnstan to keep relaying."

Aelfraed glanced across the room, even closer to the hole he could get a good look at the rune between the boards of the ceiling and floor. Each floor board was scratched and nails had been pulled up. O'Darachir pulled up a board. The dust and insulating materials that he expected to see were missing. The bare wood was marked with burnt black ink that flowed past the board and further under the floor. Whatever the rune was it was big.

"I think I need to see more," Aelfraed said, it wasn't clear as it was. Mostly just flow lines with little in the way of symbols to give that flow purpose.

O'Darachir nodded. He started work pulling up the boards. Each one was set on the bed. Aelfraed joined him while Iorwerth's hand became the only light source. He moved as best he could while standing on the beams between the floorboards to keep it somewhere useful for them.

**

Eventually once they removed most of the boards not covered by the furniture at the sides of the room they could see the whole of the rune that remained in the room. The flow lines spiralled out from the centre and split into smaller spirals. Along the way were symbols designed to slow the flow. At the end of each spiral was a symbol that looked like the one on the wall downstairs that would have brought magical energy to the light runes. While he couldn't see the completed spiral as it would have looked above the lights he had a good idea of what it was for even if he didn't know the specifics.

"That is bigger than I expected all these flow lines. Looks like a timer of some kind," O'Darachir said.

"Yes, but there are no guidance runes to keep the magic attuned. Unless they were at the centre then all this was meant to do is take in magical energy and slowly intensify it until it reached the runes below and overloaded them," Aelfraed rambled as he looked over the extra spirals.

Crude really but basic enough that it could have been anyone that understood the basics of magic flow. Looking at it he doubted that O'Darachir would have needed him at all.

"This can't have been quick, or discreet to make," O'Darachir said thoughtfully, "though setting it off would have been if they knew which boards to take up."

"Emmett must have been sneaking in here then. None of us used it so we wouldn't have seen," Iorwerth said.

"Not if he was also working. To have moved all this stuff, the floor boards and then drawn the spiral? Unlikely that he could have done that without his absence from work being noticed," O'Darachir said taking another glance around the room, "if it was him then he had an accomplice."

Chapter Thirteen

They headed back down with O'Darachir keeping a closer watch on Iorwerth. Aelfraed thought it was unlikely but figured it fit with the man's caution of not acting until there was evidence.

"Unless one of you was working with him. It wasn't Emmett," O'Darachir announced as he stepped back into the room, eying the various faces.

Magnolia's head whipped up, "how... how dare... how can you think it was one of us," she said shaking.

Iorwerth stumbled in shock, "wait, what? That's what you were thinking!"

"You can't be serious, what brought this on?" Alexander asked.

"Unfortunately I am. The runes Aelfraed noticed are rather extensive. The furniture has been moved and the floor boards pulled up. In less than a week it would be impossible for Emmett to have done without an accomplice," O'Darachir explained.

"There has to be another explanation, none of us would have worked with him," Elouise spoke up.

"I already told you it wasn't me," Emmett protested.

"Well there are only three people that have that sort of access, unless you three are here that often. And alone," O'Darachir said looking expectantly for confirmation.

There was a long uncomfortable silence as O'Darachir looked from face to face. Elouise shifted to stand more between him and Celia but didn't leave Magnolia's side. Alexander gripped his cane hard enough to make his knuckles go white. He was shaking his head.

"No you can't, you can't think it was me! I loved him," Magnolia sobbed.

Alexander moved between them, "you have to be wrong. She wouldn't, Iorwerth wouldn't. Look at them both. Do they look like they had anything to do with this?" Alexander asked firmly.

"Agh it was Maggie!" Emmett shouted drawing everyone's attention, "I saw her. Not doing the stabbing but working on the runes. That's how I knew they were there. I'd seen the like before. I thought if I used it I'd still get paid too. They'd think I wasn't connected to the break in. I was planning to be found in a cupboard or something. She must have taken chance," he insisted, frantically trying to back up his own statements.

"No... no... no. I didn't! I wouldn't! I told you, I loved him!" she sobbed.

Iorwerth clenched his fists, "the way you two argued didn't sound like it," he snapped.

Her head shot round, "Iorwerth!" She shrieked, "I loved him... I wouldn't... how could you think I didn't."

"You argued? About what?" Wynnstan asked.

"Money, me, time spent, anything really," Iorwerth listed.

She shook her head, a franticness to it. Muttering under her breath.

"Told you it was her," Emmett said straining against his cuffs.

"She wouldn't, there has to be a more reasonable explanation. Magnolia, please, what happened," Alexander pressed.

"I... I didn't... I didn't kill him. It... it wasn't... I drew the runes. I did that much but I swear I didn't kill him. That wasn't even for today. I just wanted him to notice me again," Magnolia was almost unable to say through tears.

"Notice you? Magnolia he loved you," Celia insisted, "surely it was just a misunderstanding."

She shook her head, "past tense. He'd lost interest. The arguments had gotten worse. I just wanted to get his attention. Be sure before

I divorced. I had no reason to kill him. The house is mine," she explained.

"Check her for any weapons," O'Darachir ordered.

"What exactly was your plan then?" Wynnstan asked and the other Wardens instructed her to stand and started searching through her pockets.

"I'd set it off next week, a dinner alone. Just us. We'd laugh it off and reconnect," she explained, "it wasn't meant to blow through the ceiling."

Her pockets were emptied out onto the table. Nothing out of the ordinary, a pen, her house keystone, a powder mirror and a fine comb.

"See, nothing. Emmett's the only one with a knife. It had to be him," Elouise glanced to the man and was trying to put herself between Magnolia and the Wardens in a defensive way.

"It doesn't rule out them working together," O'Darachir said, "hit man does pay more than thief."

"No, no it wasn't me. I swear!" Panic rising in his voice.

It was possible but thinking about how they had been before and during dinner Aelfraed couldn't believe it. He couldn't help but glance to where Magnolia had been sitting, next to where Giselbert had been sat. They had hidden the distance well. He shuddered when were the body had been came into view accidentally. He was thankful that the body itself had been removed while they had been gone. Leaving only blood drying on the wooden floor and the hastily drawn rune that had been meant to save him.

It still wasn't something he wanted to look at. He quickly averted his eyes. For a long moment it picked at his brain. His eyes drawn back.

"This is wrong," Aelfraed said as it dawned on him that the rune didn't match his father's instructions.

"What?" Wynnstan asked looking over.

"The rune circle… it's wrong. These runes are all off," Aelfraed explained pointing out what didn't match to what it should have been.

"Did it get interfered with it by the blood?" Wynnstan asked.

"No, this is wrong. This is all wrong," Aelfraed replied.

"Don't be ridiculous, do you even pay attention in your classes?" His father brushed him off, "any mistake was clearly yours."

Aelfraed shied away, "I... no... I wasn't involved in this and they are wrong. I'm sure of it."

"No they're not we did exactly what Mr Agmundrson said," Celia defended, "unless he's not as competent as he keeps acting."

"Are you questioning me? I guided them through it! I think I know better than you," his father turned on him, face red, "all of you!"

He shot pointed glares at Aelfraed and then at Celia for daring to insinuate he didn't know what he was talking about. Aelfraed had no doubt the man was on the edge of not being able to regain any kind of composure at this point.

"Father just look at it," Aethelric insisted.

"What would you know, you would barely pick up a book on the subject," he snapped at Aethelric.

"Ugh just look at it already," Caiomhe roughly grabbed his arm and pulled him over, "stubborn mule," she muttered.

"I don't need to! It's correct; of course it is... what is that?" He started to insist before his eyes fell on it.

"Just how far wrong is this thing?" O'Darachir asked.

"Wrong enough that it would counter any healing spell cast in it," their father stated.

"That would require some expertise wouldn't it," O'Darachir asked.

"It would," Aelfraed nodded.

"Yet you claim to have walked them through it? Are you sure you instructed right?" O'Darachir asked Aelfraed's father.

"Yes, what else are you insinuating!" The man snapped.

"I may not be an expert but that definitely isn't what he said," Celia said finally venturing over with Elouise away from the cluster around Magnolia.

"Who drew the circle?" Wynnstan asked.

"Iorwerth, Celia and Elouise," Aethelric said.

"We were under a lot of pressure. It was probably just a mistake. Iorwerth was in shock more than the rest of us," Elouise explained.

"It took all my focus to even follow the instructions," Iorwerth confirmed.

"And make it a counter circle accidentally?" O'Darachir dug.

"I... I guess not," Elouise stumbled over her words.

"No! They wouldn't!" Magnolia protested, "they had no reason to!"

"No offense but this is awful complicated to do off the cuff. It couldn't have been just anyone," Aelfraed pointed out.

"True, any experts amongst the three?" O'Darachir asked looking more to Alexander at this point. Pointedly ignoring Magnolia.

Alexander frowned, "not in that. Iorwerth has some training in transmutation but I don't know how much that would help."

"Then they must have had something to work from," Wynnstan commented, "could they have memorized it in advance?"

"Why would we need to? We didn't even know Mr Agmundrson was coming!" Elouise defended.

"Aunty could have told you," Iorwerth said, "she invited him weeks ago."

"That didn't mean I knew he would come. I only invited him because Giselbert wanted him here. They were friends even if I didn't understand it. I invited his friend because I wanted him to be happy," Magnolia insisted, "I didn't want him dead."

"Seriously this is ridiculous. Why even try if there was a chance Mr Agmundrson would even be there," Elouise ranted.

"Why not? Emmett for one. Someone to take the blame while the rest of you look like the robbed innocents," O'Darachir said with a raised brow, "not that ridiculous. Search the three of them."

**
*

Their pockets were emptied out onto the floor. Elouise's pockets were rather deep due to being under her dress rather than in it. Celia carried less. Iorwerth had only a small number of things in his.

Amongst the things from Elouise and Celia was their keystones, purses, a fountain pen and Celia's watch. Iorwerth didn't have a keystone, likely kept somewhere in the house. He also had a fountain pen the cap having gone astray and a slip of paper with a rune hastily drawn on in. A little wobbly and the paper spotted with blood.

"What's this?" O'Darachir asked turning the paper over and examining both the runes and the blood. He glanced over to the one on the floor.

Aelfraed looked between the two. They were different even when discarding the areas where they had been drawn to his father's instructions. Symbols that indicated a change in shape were familiar from his studies but the more precise ones that declared what was changing and to what were not.

"Looks like something for transmutation," Aelfraed said leaning over to look at the note.

"It's just something from my studies. Must have gotten blood on it during the incident," Iorwerth explained, "it's nothing."

"I'll decide that," O'Darachir said, "what is this for? Why would you have this at dinner?"

"Just a reminder, I was reading a bit before dinner and needed to make a note. It's just a reference for later," he explained.

"Can you confirm that this wouldn't have been any use in the incident?" O'Darachir asked Aelfraed, "I'm not sure I can trust his word."

Aelfraed shook his head, "I recognise some of it but not enough to know what it was for. It might even have nothing to do with this. It's nothing like the changes to the one on the floor."

"It has nothing to do with it because I didn't do anything," Iorwerth defended.

"Huh isn't that the symbol for metal?" Caoimhe asked stepping closer to get a better look, "what were you reading about?"

"You know this?" Wynnstan asked.

"Not completely, that symbol in the rune and a few of the others look like the ones used to change the printing plates. The ones used to replicate the photos," she explained.

"So it would change metal?" O'Darachir asked.

"Should do, pretty rough though. Doubt it would get anything detailed done," Caoimhe said.

Rough, Aelfraed thought about the word. He recalled the rough shaped broken assumed candle holder on the table. The wobbly lines. A realisation dawned on him, that those dips and ridges were the prints of fingers. Prints from someone grabbing and shaping the object.

"It's not a candle holder," Aelfraed realised.

"What's not a candle holder?" Wynnstan asked.

"This," Aelfraed said moving over to the table and pointing to the item, "I thought it was a candle holder that broke or some odd ornament but it seemed rather rough to be an ornament. It's been hand shaped and roughly."

Magnolia scoffed, "I wouldn't have put something like that on the table. Giselbert wouldn't have either."

"I definitely didn't set it on the table, would have pocketed it, given the chance," Emmett said craning his head to get a good look at it, "looks pure silver and wouldn't have been missed as much as the cutlery."

"Our missing knife perhaps?" O'Darachir asked.

Aelfraed's father frowned approaching the table, he uttered a few words of a spell. One not really designed for the task but would do the job. Aelfraed recognised it as one used to locate blood and veins.

"There's blood incorporated into the metal," he said with a slight smugness on his face. Probably soothing his ego through his ability to help finally.

Iorwerth's fist clenched as eyes landed on him. There was a growing look of horror on Magnolia's face as he looked down to avoid her eyes.

"No... no you didn't," Magnolia stared, "please tell me you didn't."

Iorwerth sighed, "I'm not getting out of this am I? Fine, I did it. I saw a chance and I took it."

"Why... why would you..." Magnolia stuttered her voice growing cold.

"Why not, he gave me plenty of reasons. You gave me plenty too. There was no waiting him out. You would never divorce him. To desperate to make amends and in the meantime he treat me like he owned me."

"Owned you? He saw you as his own son!" she shrieked.

"Phft, you and I clearly see that differently. Surely you saw, saw how he was when I didn't do what he wanted. I disobeyed him and then he wanted to ship me of to who knows where. Don't think you're any better. You did it too," he ranted.

Magnolia stood quickly, her legs almost crumpling out from under her for a moment. She rushed forward only to be held back by Wynnstan and another Warden. The rest making moves to detain Iorwerth and keep the other guests from acting.

"Take them both down to the keep," O'Darachir instructed nodding in the direction of both Iorwerth and Emmett, "we'll deal with the rest there."

Chapter Fourteen

Aelfraed dragged his feet as they walked back towards the Rune Step. While he just wanted to get back and crash in his borrowed bed he also didn't really want to face the Step for a second time. He was always going to have to but that desire was even less so now. If he didn't feel like he'd drop before he got there he would have considered walking all the way back to Aethelric's.

The Step was deserted of the crowds of earlier; the late night had passed on into the earliest of morning hours. His eyes still on the ground he headed for the Step they had used before. He just wanted to sleep before his father would drag him out of the bed in the early hours of the morning to head back to Edinburgh. Sleep as much as he could before being forced to inevitable face the longer Step right before morning lectures. He'd probably still have to attend too, no matter how bad he felt.

His father snatched his arm and started to lead him away to another Step. He stumbled at the unexpected movement.

"What are you doing?" Aethelric asked rushing over to keep pace.

"Where on earth are you going? The Step's this way," Caoimhe gestured where they had been heading, "I know I said find somewhere else but at this point I think we all just want to sleep."

"Back to Edinburgh," their father stated plainly as he continued to walk towards the Step that would take them to Central and on to the intercity Steps.

"What!" Caoimhe snapped.

"Tonight? Surely the morning would be better," Aethelric said.

"I have a morning lecture to get back for and I am not leaving Aelfraed here," he scowled picking up the pace. Once again talking as if he wasn't there. As if he was a child in need of supervision.

Tonight was too soon, way too soon. He didn't want to go back yet. Maybe the morning might have been better but now he was thinking about it, he didn't want to go back at all. His father paused as Aelfraed pulled his arm from his grip. He was so expectant that Aelfraed would do as he wanted that he didn't even turn back to look until Aethelric caught up again.

"He was already intending to go back at least let him get some sleep first," Aelthelric complained.

"And risk him stumbling into more trouble? Or being late when you try to argue over it in the morning? We're going tonight," he grabbed Aelfraed's arm again and started pulling him away.

Aelfraed stopped, his father turned back to look at him. He pulled his arm out of the grip. His father expected him just to fold under the pressure. He didn't want to do that anymore. He didn't have to do that anymore. He was here and not there. All he had to do was say it. That wasn't an easy task.

"What do you think you are doing?" His father scowled at him. That red from earlier in the evening creeping easily back onto his face.

He almost didn't want to speak, "I'm not going," Aelfraed said quietly.

"Not going? I won't stand for this foolishness! I've had enough of your trouble making for tonight!" His voice rose drawing the attention of the few still using the Step at this time of night, "we are going back now, and that's final."

He reached for Aelfraed's arm but he moved back, "no, I'm staying."

"You expect me to believe that you'd turn up tomorrow morning without my interference?" He gave a condescending laugh through his clenched teeth.

"That... that isn't what I meant... I'm not going back," Aelfraed corrected awkwardly.

"What! Don't be foolish you have studies to complete! You'll never be anything if you don't!" He ranted, no longer seeming to care who was watching.

"What's the point of being anything when I don't even know what I want to be?" Aelfraed asked.

"Yes you do! You're going to be a physician," the man looked at him like he had grown a second head.

Aelfraed shook his head. "No, you wanted that... I didn't know what I wanted. Maybe I will be but not if this is the way it has to happen. I can't take it anymore, being under your thumb."

"That's what you call it? My help when you can barely keep up! Fine! Sink! Maybe then you'll see how much you need me!" He bellowed before storming off towards the Step alone.

Aelfraed sighed, he could feel his legs shaking underneath him. He'd done it. He tried not to listen to the part of his brain that was saying his father was right. That he'd come crawling back. He wouldn't. He couldn't, not after that. Well not unless he wanted to never be let out of sight again.

Aethelric's hand landed on his shoulder and pulled him into a hug.

"Let's go home," Aethelric said with a comforting smile on his face.

He shifted awkwardly, "is that still okay... I might be there a bit longer than planned," he didn't want to impose on them. He should have asked before he did that.

Aethelric smiled, "as I said, as long as you need Aelfie."

Aelfraed looked to Caoimhe for confirmation. He didn't think she would disagree but he had to be sure.

"You're always welcome," she smiled before gesturing in the direction of their Step.

The A Curiosity Piqued Series will continue in 2024 with:

The Medallion Heist

There is an interesting exhibit opening at a museum in Newcastle, unfortunately during the opening night celebrations an item is stolen and they are coming back for the centrepiece... the very cursed centrepiece.

Have I piqued your curiosity? Find out more at

"Seriously you just won't quit." He groaned as Aelfraed cut him off again.

"Hand it over."

"Not happening, these things are going to net us a very pretty penny."

"Great you're getting paid..." Aelfraed groaned, "you realise how dangerous that is right?" The gloves on his hands said yes but the casual way it hung from his fingers said otherwise.

"I'm not stupid," he snapped. That insinuation hit home. Aelfraed had a bad feeling something had happened with the first medallion.

"Please, hand it over before someone gets hurt."

"Not a chance. You want it back you're going to have to catch me," he taunted before barrelling towards the edge of the building and leaping into the air.

This snippet is a work in progress and may change between now and the release of Medallion Heist.

Supporters

These awesome people supported me during the writing of this book through my Twitch, Patreon or Ko-fi.

TentuTesla, Vrastorna, Azraelle_Studios, Emperor Kiallitch, TheBigJucy89, MsIriala, AtlantiaKing, StrangeLace, visi0nsh0t, bigfootbjornsen, AnimaCores, CeciliumStar, TomWeasley, BrenNailedIt, InigoGarcia, sun_berry, thedarlingwordsmith, Sientir, EricRonin, TenPint, Itadakimasu1995, MadaoMike, Sarett, NaksterAkai, Jenny2point0, BeePanda, Chocolatecitysim, mrsfuturejervistetch106, mountainshade1, wiktorjus, Mickyanne123

Thank you all!

The World Primer

About the world

The world of A Curiosity Piqued is a place like our own world except magic has been around since the dawn of time. Humans learnt to use and harness the magic creating changes in history, technology and culture.

In the present of the story the setting has reached an industrial era that is equivalent to the Victorian era. There has been a string of new inventions most of which use magic on an industrial scale.

Introducing a slightly familiar Newcastle in the north of what in our world would have been Britain. Instead without our expected visit from the Romans Pretani is a series of allied kingdoms with more Celtic and Nordic origins.

Wondering what happened to the Romans? They still existed just didn't get as far out of the Mediterranean with the addition of older cultures with a greater grasp of magic giving them some trouble.

This all sets up a Newcastle that is both familiar and unfamiliar. With buildings that were constructed the same as in our world but with the addition of magic changing the technology and the culture around them.

How Magic Works

While you don't need to know how magic works going into this story because what you need to know is in the text but I know if you are like me you are interested in the world building. So here's a quick little primer to how magic works in this world as is currently understood by its residents.

Magic is the use of language and tools to manipulate reality through the use of an energy generated from molecules that build up in organic materials. Living things process these molecules specifically from their food and use them in magic.

Any casting of magic requires the use of language, any language works as long as there is also thought and intention behind the language. As long as someone has the energy stored and the knowledge of how something works they can use magic. For example a person needs to know how the body works and heals in order to use magic to accelerate the process.

Runes come up a lot in this story they function as a written way to store a spell. Saving focus and time. Often they are used to cast spells that would be cast over and over or more complicated spells. For clarity a rune is used as a general term for any writing or symbols used to store magic energy or cast predetermined spells rather than a specific form of writing like Futhark (Nordic runes). Though they do sometimes incorporate some traditional runes in the symbols created for older spells. They are varied and specific to the spell. Often even to the target of the spell. Like technology in our own world there is often a lot of research going into making these runes smaller and more efficient to use.

A Name Guide

Aelfraed – ael(ale) fr aed(aid)
Aethelric – Ae th el ric
Caoimhe – Kee va
Alvis – Al vis
Agmundrson – A g m un der son
Caron – Ca rone
Stirgsen – St ier g sen
O'Darachir – O' D ara ch ir
Odell – o dehl
Giselbert – G is el bert
Iowerth – Y orr werr th